Summer with My Cowboy

Summer with My Cowboy

LINDA LAEL MILLER

MAISEY YATES

kensingtonbooks.com

KENSINGTON BOOKS are published by

Kensington Publishing Corp.
900 Third Avenue
New York, NY 10022

ISBN: 978-1-4967-5657-2
ISBN: 978-1-4967-5658-9 (ebook)

First Kensington Trade Edition: May 2026

10 9 8 7 6 5 4 3 2 1

Printed in the United States of America

The authorized representative in the EU for product safety and compliance
is eucomply OU, Parnu mnt 139b-14, Apt 123
Tallinn, Berlin 11317, hello@eucompliancepartner.com

Contents

Cowboy Wanted

LINDA LAEL MILLER

For Wendy and Jeremy with love

Prologue

Eighteen months earlier
Seattle, Washington

Kendra winced and closed her eyes as the judge's gavel struck his desktop with a loud *crack*.

Her marriage was over.

Her dreams of a home and a happy family were dashed, forever.

The liars had won.

Kendra's divorce attorney and good friend, Carla Helms, laid a gentle hand on her forearm and whispered, "You're going to be all right. Let's get out of here—without giving *them* the satisfaction of watching you fall apart in front of God and everybody, okay?"

Them. That would be her ex-husband Ethan's mother, Desuma—almost certainly meaning "decimate"—and his stepsister, Elyse.

For reasons Kendra had never fully understood, those two

women absolutely *despised* her, and they had, from the moment Ethan had brought her to meet them at the family mansion on Mercer Island, two years before.

Oh, they'd been polite enough then, Desuma and Elyse, but Kendra had immediately sensed that it was a façade, and a cold storm of resentment roared behind it, gaining power with every passing moment.

Ethan hadn't seemed to notice their carefully controlled hostility that day, and later, when Kendra raised the subject, hoping for reassurance, he had laughingly accused her of being "oversensitive." And that was the way it went, from then on.

In hindsight, that first red flag had swelled to the size of a city skyline.

Now, as Kendra got to her feet and turned to follow Carla out of the courtroom, she kept her eyes averted, so that pair of witches couldn't look into them and see just how much pain they'd caused her. They were probably high on their victory.

Since the case had been a civil one, there weren't a lot of onlookers, a fact for which Kendra was grateful—until she crashed directly into Ethan on the way out.

Somehow, he'd gotten between her and Carla, and now he was holding her by the shoulders.

She refused to look up into his face, but not because she'd been crying during the hearing. Oh, no. What she felt in that instant was fury.

She'd loved this man once, loved him more than life, looked forward to building a family with him—the more kids, the better.

But now, *now* she felt only a surge of outrage and injustice.

So much for feeling crushed and broken, at least for the moment.

"Please get out of my way," she said icily. She tried to shrug free, but his grasp only tightened.

Ethan Larkin, a handsome, well-built man with brown eyes and a normally winsome smile, actually had the nerve to *grin* at her. The effect was like a slap in the face.

"Now, now," he said, almost crooning the words, "there's no need to be hostile, is there? You're receiving a generous settlement—which is more than you deserve, after cheating on me. And if you're civil, I might even let you see Walter once a year or so."

Walter was Ethan's golden retriever, and Kendra felt a pang of sorrow at the sound of his name. She would miss that sweet, funny dog for the rest of her life.

"What do you want, Ethan?" she asked, after a sigh of weary impatience.

"I want to know if you plan to marry Charlie Baker, now that our divorce is final. That would make sense, wouldn't it? Since you slept with him behind my back and got yourself pregnant in the process?"

Kendra felt heat surge into her face, and sorrow landed in the pit of her stomach with the weight of an anvil. "I didn't cheat on you," she said. "And you know it."

Charlie was literally just a friend. A co-worker at the firm where Kendra had worked long before she met Ethan.

There had been no affair, and the child she'd lost by miscarriage after only three months of pregnancy had been Ethan's, not Charlie's or anyone else's.

Thanks to the dedicated efforts of Desuma and Elyse, however, Ethan had taken the lies as gospel, even after a DNA test proving he was the lost infant's biological father. He'd claimed the test had been faked, and there was no convincing him otherwise.

Kendra had fallen hard for the wrong man, and she was inwardly shattered from the whole experience, but that didn't mean she was stupid.

Misguided, maybe.

Gullible, for sure.

But definitely not stupid.

Ethan was glaring down at her. "*Liar,*" he rasped.

Just then, Desuma and Elyse appeared at his sides, looking vaguely creepy, for all their branded clothes and expensive makeup and over-the-top jewelry.

In fact, they resembled ghouls, at least in Kendra's opinion.

And they were all triumph.

The urge to knock out some of their ridiculously white teeth was overwhelming, but Kendra managed to curb it. She was not a violent person, after all.

It was then that Carla shouldered her way into the little cluster, putting herself between Ethan and the Sea Sirens, and Kendra.

"This conversation is over," she said, and even though Carla was petite, her voice and manner conveyed authority, and the unholy trio drew back. "Ms. Spencer has things to attend to."

With that, she took hold of Kendra's elbow and virtually dragged her out of the small courtroom, across the waiting area and out into the overcast gloom of Seattle in March.

Neither woman spoke during the walk to the parking lot and their cars.

Carla would be heading straight for her office, where piles of work probably awaited her.

Kendra, on the other hand, had no particular destination in mind. At least, not for the moment.

Standing beside her plain, practical blue sedan, Kendra looked up at the thousand shades of gray filling the sky. And she sighed, as though a new weight had settled upon her shoulders.

She'd been born and raised in the sunny state of Arizona, and the contrast had been a challenge ever since she'd come to Seattle, straight out of college, to take a job at Amazon.

"What are you thinking?" Carla asked, the keys to her car, a flashy Corvette, dangling from a metal loop on her handbag.

"I'm thinking—" Kendra answered, after a few moments of consideration, as a smile gathered on her lips, "I'm thinking of going home to Copper Ridge."

Chapter 1

The Hot N Tot Diner
Copper Ridge, Arizona

Another day, another dollar, Kendra reflected with a sigh and a smile as she tied her apron strings and surveyed the over-crowded café where she would spend the next several hours serving meals to both locals and tourists.

Compared to her previous salary, her wages as a waitress were minimal—but, then, she wasn't there for the money any-way. For her, working in the diner was a way of getting out of her own head, laughing and talking with living human beings instead of staring bleakly at images on a phone or computer screen.

It was, in short, a way of staying sane.

When she'd first returned to her hometown, a year and a half before, she'd been an emotional wreck, to say the least. Her divorce from Ethan Larkin had pulled the proverbial rug out from under her feet, not because there was anything left of the love she'd felt for him before, but because he'd upended her entire life.

And she'd been especially vulnerable when her marriage fell apart, because she'd so recently lost the child she'd yearned for, prayed for, and cherished practically from conception.

Now that some time had passed, and she no longer had to contend with Desuma and Elyse, or with Ethan himself, she was stronger.

Happier.

She did miss Walter though.

Maybe, she reflected, not for the first time, she should get a dog of her own.

She might, after she'd adjusted to the seismic shift in her circumstances.

For one thing, she was still getting used to living in a small town again instead of a major city. Although Copper Ridge was basically the same modest, close-knit community she'd known growing up, no place stayed the same forever.

There were lots of new people in Copper Ridge now, while many of her childhood friends had grown up and left. She was still adapting to that, too.

When she'd first arrived, she'd hidden out in her late grandmother's guest house, a pleasant little cottage behind the massive—and empty—family home, but she soon realized she needed to get out and breathe fresh air more often, to interact with others instead of surfing the internet for hours on end, stalking Ethan, Desuma and Elyse on social media, and scrolling through dozens of photos on her phone.

Every one of those captured moments stung her deeply—especially those of Walter, Ethan's dog, frolicking in the surf in front of the Larkins' beach-front home on Mercer Island.

Kendra drew a deep breath and centered herself in the present moment.

It was time to focus on the tasks at hand.

She had work to do.

Armed with a smile and a pot of freshly brewed coffee, she began making the rounds, refilling cups at multiple tables and exchanging pleasantries as she went.

After that, she greeted and seated new arrivals, taking their orders, rushing full and empty plates to and from the kitchen.

It was a blessedly ordinary day.

Until the front door swung open and Gage Elder walked in, that is.

There was nothing ordinary about *him*.

He'd just moved to Copper Ridge—probably from Hollywood—a month before, and, with his vivid blue-green eyes, longish sandy hair and lean, muscular build, he was a sight to behold.

Everyone in town knew he was a champion bronc-rider, having claimed fancy silver buckle after fancy silver buckle at the National Finals Rodeo—the NFR—in Las Vegas, year upon year. On top of that, he worked as a stuntman and had appeared in countless movies and TV shows, acting as a stand-in for a number of legendary actors.

It was impossible not to be affected by that lopsided smile of his, never mind the rest of him.

Now, his azure gaze locked with Kendra's as he held the door for a woman around his age and a teenage girl, and he gave a slight—almost imperceptible—nod of greeting.

After recovering her equilibrium, Kendra greeted the new arrivals pleasantly and led them to a table beside a window.

Politeness personified, Gage Elder drew back a chair for the woman, then for the girl, before seating himself.

According to the rumor mill, which was well-oiled in Copper Ridge, the new guy in town was single, a widower, to be exact.

But Kendra, who had decided not to allow herself to be attracted to him under any circumstances whatsoever, hadn't missed the fact that the woman who accompanied him was drop-dead gorgeous—and very comfortable in his presence.

The young girl, for her part, resembled him so closely that she might well have been his daughter.

All of which underscored Kendra's belief that, as attractive as the cowboy/stuntman was, she didn't dare allow herself to be interested in him *at all.*

Even though he'd subtly flirted with her on two previous occasions—first, when they'd encountered each other in the aisle of the local bookstore and he'd smiled, introduced himself and struck up a casual conversation, and second, when he'd come into the diner for breakfast a week before and straight-out asked her if she'd like to join him for dinner and a movie sometime soon.

She'd politely refused, offering an excuse she couldn't recall now, even as she took their initial order for beverages and silently prayed that the heat she felt surging along the length of her neck to pound in her cheeks didn't actually show.

When he'd asked her out, every primal instinct she possessed had screamed, *Yes, yes, yes.*

But her common sense had said otherwise.

She'd been attracted to Ethan Larkin in the same incomprehensibly crazy, fundamental way, and look how *that* had turned out.

In the end, she'd lost everything, including her confidence in her own judgment.

Kendra simply could not trust herself to choose a man who wouldn't eventually destroy her.

It was crazy, she knew that.

But knowing changed nothing.

Kendra Spencer meant to stay safely single for the rest of her life.

The cowboy's eyes had a glint of gentle understanding—and

amusement—as he looked up from the menu. "What's the special today?" he asked.

He'd noticed that she was blushing, for sure.

Kendra swallowed hard, once, twice, a third time, and then managed, somehow, to answer. "Country fried chicken, mashed potatoes and creamed corn," she blurted out.

But she was thinking, *Forget food. You, Mr. Elder, are special. All* too *special.*

Forgetting his plan to be subtle, Gage watched openly as Kendra hurried away, toward the counter and the kitchen beyond.

She was a mystery to him, not because she'd sidestepped his attempts to get acquainted with her—plenty of women had done that over the years—but because there was so much going on behind that may-I-help-you? smile.

Confidence, counterbalanced by fear.

Innate happiness, coupled with a fathomless sort of sorrow.

He wanted to ask Kendra Spencer a thousand-and-one questions but, even more than that, he wanted to hold her. And it wasn't about sex. At least, not yet.

He huffed out a sigh and turned back to his tablemates.

As soon as Gage's thirteen-year-old niece Brittany excused herself and left the table to visit the restroom, his sister Sophie leaned forward and whispered, with a benevolent smirk, "So that's the woman you mentioned before? The one who won't give you the time of day?"

Gage set his jaw, relaxed it again. Sophie was three years older than he was, and even though they were both adults, she still liked to play the big sister.

Momentarily, he regretted confiding that he was attracted to Kendra, the skittish waitress with the beautiful blue eyes and light auburn hair.

"It shouldn't surprise you to learn," he replied, resting his forearms on the tabletop and leaning in a little to show he wasn't intimidated, "that I'm not the kind of guy who evaluates people through the lens of my male ego."

Sophie, a lovely brunette who'd recently married a nice guy named Hunter Pembroke after years as a divorcée, was happier than Gage had ever seen her, and Brittany, her daughter, seemed to be adjusting well, too.

All of which made him happy, though it brought a pang of sadness because any reference to marriage brought his late wife, Summer, to mind. She'd died in a car crash six years before, and taken a chunk of Gage's soul with her when she left.

They hadn't had a chance to start a family of their own.

They hadn't even had a chance to say good-bye.

In fact, their last conversation had been an argument. A stupid one that Gage couldn't even remember now.

After all that time, the guilt still stung.

Nowadays, Sophie and Brittany were all that was left of his family, since the folks had both passed over during the pandemic, not of Covid, but of congestive heart failure—Dad first, then a few months later, Mom.

"Hey," Sophie said, studying his face, "I wasn't accusing you of being an egomaniac, Bro."

"I know," Gage replied, sighing the words as much as saying them.

Kendra returned just then, with their drinks.

Gage kept his eyes on the scratched Formica tabletop.

For some crazy reason, his heartbeat had picked up speed, pounding hard at the base of his throat.

"Thank you," Sophie told Kendra, in cheerful tones.

"The food will be out soon," Kendra responded, politely but coolly.

Brittany returned to the table, waited at a little distance while Kendra hurried away again.

Gage sighed. Did Kendra think he was fixing to grab her or something?

"Talk to Kendra," Sophie urged quietly. "Find a way."

Brittany clearly hadn't overheard, or she would have added her two cents to the conversation. The girl had freshened her lip gloss and brushed her shoulder-length blonde hair to a high shine, and her eyes were alight with joy.

She loved visiting her "favorite"—and only—uncle, and now that she and her mom were about to head back to Phoenix, she was brimming with things she wanted to get said before they left.

"This is a great town!" she proclaimed, looking around the crowded café before settling into her vinyl-covered chair again and reaching for her tall glass of lemonade. "But I don't get why you decided to live in a double-wide, Uncle G. You could build a real house, after all. A big one, like you had when you and—and—when you lived in Santa Fe, I mean—"

Color rose to Brittany's cheeks and pulsed there.

"I'm sorry," she whispered.

Sophie reached over to squeeze her daughter's hand in reassurance, but it was Gage who spoke.

"It's okay to mention Summer's name, Brittany," he said, his voice a little hoarse. "She's been gone for a while now."

"You're not over her, though, right?" Like her mother, Brittany had been waiting for Gage to meet someone new, start a family, and live happily ever after.

Her cornflower-blue eyes were still shining with tears.

"I'll never get over Summer," Gage responded.

An awkward silence fell.

Kendra returned with their food a few moments later, asked the usual routine questions—did anyone want a refill on their beverages? Extra ketchup or mustard?

When everyone shook their head no, she fled again.

"You *like* her," Brittany told her uncle in a conspiratorial whisper.

Gage used the hand sanitizer Sophie had produced from her handbag and sighed. Set the little plastic bottle back on the tabletop with a slight *thump*. "Never mind who I like or don't like," he told his niece, picking up his bacon-cheeseburger in one hand. "And what's wrong with living in a double-wide? It's pretty nice inside, isn't it?"

Brittany had managed to blink back her tears by then, but she was clearly still anxious to mend any fences that might have been broken by her previous remark.

"It's really nice," she replied eagerly. "The kitchen is a-maz-ing!" She paused, frowned slightly. "But what if you decide to get married again? Maybe even have some kids? There won't be very much elbow room in that place when it's not just you and Stanley."

Stanley was Gage's dog, a combination Irish setter and Labrador retriever.

As usual, Gage felt a momentary stab of regret for leaving his furry pal home alone.

"Look," he said quietly, "I understand that you mean well, both of you. But this matchmaking thing is starting to get under my hide."

Sophie slanted a glance in Kendra's direction and cleared her throat, but she said nothing.

Brittany, never at a loss for words it seemed, replied with a frustrated sigh, a slight shake of her head and, "You're not getting any younger, you know."

That made Gage laugh, which was a major relief. "I'll be thirty-five in October," he pointed out, "but I guess from the viewpoint of a thirteen-year-old, I'm approaching codgerhood."

"I'm almost *fourteen*," Brittany pointed out. "I'm going to be in *high school* this year. Next thing you know, I'll be totally grown-up!"

After that, things lightened up.

Eyes glowing, Sophie talked about her business-partner-turned-husband, Hunter, and the start-up marketing firm they were building together. There were plenty of challenges, she admitted, but the bottom line was in good shape.

When the meal ended, Gage paid the bill, over Sophie's protests, silently marveling at the fact that Kendra's presence just west of his right elbow made his nerves vibrate.

At some point, he was going to have to man up and try again, but given her resistance, it seemed wiser to give things some time to develop—or not.

Stealing one last glance at Kendra before he followed his sister and niece out of the diner, Gage opened Sophie's car door and waited for her to take a seat behind the wheel.

"When are you coming to visit us?" his sister asked, putting on her seat belt.

Across from her, in the passenger seat, Brittany did the same. She was leaning forward a little, in order to see around her mother.

Remarkably, she didn't chime in.

"When I can," Gage answered, noncommittal. Between monitoring his investments and looking after a horse and a dog, he had his hands full, at least for the time being.

"You'll talk to—what was her name?" Sophie asked.

As if she'd forgotten.

"Kendra," Gage answered, somewhat wearily. "For now, I plan to leave her alone. I don't want her thinking I'm a stalker or something."

"You? A stalker?" his sister countered merrily. "With all the women hoping to rope you in?"

"Good-bye," Gage replied pointedly. "And be safe on the road, please."

Sophie didn't start up her car until he'd climbed into his truck and brought the engine back to life.

Gage watched as his sister pulled out of the diner's gravel parking lot and turned south.

Then, feeling like a damn fool, he sat there for another ten minutes or so, torn between going back into the diner and asking Kendra out *again* and just heading home, where he had chores to do and spreadsheets to go over.

In the end, he stuck to his initial plan and went home.

He had work to do.

Chapter 2

By the end of that day's shift at the diner, Kendra's feet were sore and she couldn't shake the image of Gage Elder, having lunch with—whom? His wife and daughter? His girlfriend and *her* daughter?

The possibilities were endless.

Why did she even care?

What the local celebrity did was his own business, and the same was true of her. Except for the celebrity part, of course.

Parking in the paved driveway of her late grandmother's monstrosity of a house, Kendra finally managed to shift her thoughts away from Elder and the strange effect he seemed to have on her senses. She fixed her attention on the huge, three-story mansion in front of her and wondered what she should do with the place.

Fix it up and sell it?

She couldn't quite bring herself to sell it. She'd grown up in Spencer House, raised by her grandmother, instead of her irresponsible parents.

Besides, the place had been in the family since well before Arizona became a state back in February of 1912.

Kendra's multi-great-grandparents, Alexander and Marietta Spencer, had come out West from Massachusetts, started a general store, and prospered from day one.

Alexander Spencer had been one of her grandmother Symphony's favorite topics of conversation. She'd kept piles of journals, letters, photographs, newspaper clippings and other ephemera, as had her mother before her.

Now, the lot of it was safely preserved by the Copper Ridge Historical Society.

Kendra was a member of that organization, though she rarely attended their meetings. Working at the café took up a lot of her time and energy and then there were the things she did online, mainly day-trading, though the bulk of her inheritance was stashed away in CDs, blue-chip stocks and other relatively safe accounts.

In truth, she was a wealthy woman.

She didn't need to work, but she was pretty sure she'd go insane if she didn't.

Thinking these thoughts, Kendra headed up the bumpy sidewalk toward the house's elaborate veranda and the giant front door.

The door was made of solid oak, and nearly six inches thick.

As Grandma Symphony used to say, there were outlaws aplenty around, when the house was built, and one couldn't be too safe, then or now.

Rather than head for the guest house, her actual abode, to do a few yoga moves, take a shower and put on shorts, sandals and a T-shirt before logging on to her laptop, Kendra decided to wander around in the big house for a little while.

Maybe she would finally decide what to do with it.

She didn't want to live there—it was too big and she'd rattle around in it like a glass marble in the bottom of a tin bucket—

plus, without her grandmother and the staff she'd employed to run the household, it had a lonely, echo-like feel to it, as though she might round a corner or enter a room and suddenly come face-to-face with some long-gone ancestor.

Not that she believed in ghosts or anything.

The big door creaked on its hinges after Kendra turned the lock and pushed it open. She stepped inside and heard it—the ticking of the tall, heavy and very ornamental grandfather's clock on the opposite side of the entryway.

A little chill tripped up and down her spine.

There are no ghosts in this house! she reminded herself.

But since the clock hadn't been wound since who-knew-when, the ticking sound added a definite creepy note.

Kendra straightened her spine, shut the door quietly behind her, and forced herself to take a step, then another, until she was standing in front of the giant clock.

Growing up, she'd loved that thing, though she'd avoided getting too close to it, lest a sudden earthquake strike and it toppled over and squashed her to a pulp.

Though a little nervous, Kendra smiled at the memory.

Had she always been paranoid?

Maybe her disastrous marriage to Ethan Larkin *hadn't* been the beginning of her mostly minor neuroses.

"Who wound you?" Kendra asked, touching the clock.

She nearly jumped out of her skin when it immediately launched into a loud rendition of the Westminster chimes, then bonged six times.

Six o'clock, she thought, quite unnecessarily, as she looked at the face of the clock.

It occurred to Kendra then that whoever had wound the thing up might still be in the house.

Would a burglar wind a clock?

It seemed unlikely but, then, the world was a very strange place at times.

"Hello?" she called out, just in case.

She nearly fainted when Eleanor Hartford emerged from the nearby parlor with a broad smile and a nod, saying, "*I* wound the clock. It's the heartbeat of this house, after all."

Kendra, still recovering from the surprise, said nothing.

Eleanor was a successful real estate agent these days, despite her advanced age, but, as a much younger woman, she'd worked for Symphony Spencer as a housekeeper and sometime cook. They had become great friends, Symphony and Eleanor, and now that Kendra's heart had slid back down out of her throat and settled into its usual place, she realized she had no reason to be surprised by the other woman's presence.

Eleanor had her own key and stopped by occasionally to check on things, just to make sure the house was still sound.

Now, she beamed at Kendra. "I'm sorry if I scared you, honey," she said. She'd been out West for many years, obviously, but a touch of a Southern drawl lingered in her voice, like a golden undercurrent. "I just came by to make sure no pipes had burst or anything like that."

Kendra smiled back at the beloved woman, one hand resting on her breastbone. "I didn't see your car out front," she said.

"That's because I parked out back, in the alley," she said. "Folks see me around here and they start thinking the house is for sale and nagging me to tell them the asking price."

"I can't sell it—Grandmother would haunt me if I did," Kendra said, with a slight sigh. "But it seems a shame to let it just sit here, going to waste, too. It could be a B-and-B or a boarding house, I suppose, or an elder care place, or even a homeless shelter—"

Eleanor's smile was still at full wattage. "Don't go fretting. When the time's right, you'll know what to do. Besides, there aren't any homeless people in Copper Ridge, as far as I know, and there are already three nursing homes in town." She paused, reached out and caught Kendra by the hand, and squeezed. "But a B-and-B, now that might just work."

"This is northern Arizona," Kendra said, stating the obvious. "We get snow in the winter; all the snowbirds prefer Phoenix and Tucson. We don't really have many tourists—other than the kind who are just passing through headed one way or the other."

"Copper Ridge is a beautiful place," Eleanor said gently. "There's skiing in the winter, and a lot of folks come to go trail-riding the rest of the year, since there are several big ranches around here. Like the one Jack O'Ballivan runs, over near Diamond Creek."

Kendra smiled. Harper O'Ballivan, Jack's wife, was a friend of hers. They'd met at book club soon after Kendra's return to her hometown and immediately connected.

In fact, Harper was one of the few people who knew about Kendra's lost baby and broken marriage. *And* her fear of giving love another chance with someone like—well—Gage Elder.

Except that he might not even be single, even though he'd asked her out.

Kendra shifted her thoughts forcefully back to the matter at hand. "It would be a lot of work, running a B-and-B," she ruminated softly.

Eleanor laughed. "Can't imagine it would be harder than working all those shifts at the Hot N Tot," she said. "And you could always hire help. Plenty of young folks around, wanting a steady job."

"I'll consider it," Kendra said, a little surprised at herself.

Maybe Harper was right, and she was overly cautious, letting the past have too much influence over her. After all, Ethan and his demonic relatives were far away, and she didn't have to deal with them anymore. Ever.

"That's good!" Eleanor cried, elated, giving Kendra a firm hug.

Somehow, that kindly embrace restored some of Kendra's self-confidence. Sure, she'd made more than her share of mistakes—who hadn't?—but now she was safe in Copper Ridge, the place she considered home.

"I've got to get on with my evening," Eleanor announced, pulling her car keys from the pocket of her pale and stylish linen jacket, which provided a lovely contrast with her smooth, dark skin. "I'm due over at Gage Elder's place. You know, that good-looking cowboy type who's been in all those movies."

Kendra's breath caught, and her heart started pounding a little.

She hoped she wasn't blushing again, because Eleanor, having known her so long, would immediately notice and follow up with a few pertinent questions.

Fortunately, Eleanor didn't seem to notice that Kendra was mildly flustered.

"Is he selling his place?" she managed to ask, trying her best to sound normal.

"No," Eleanor said, with another smile and a shake of her head. Her hair was still dark and shiny. "No, he's looking to buy the ranch adjoining his property. You know, the old Macabee outfit? The Macabees are moving to California to live near their three daughters. Tending all those cattle and horses is too much for them, according to John. He wants his wife to live an easier life, now that they're both older."

Kendra knew the Macabees from way back. They were good, hardworking people. Maybe *too* hardworking, given that they had to be in their early to mid-eighties by now.

"So I guess Mr. Elder plans to stick around a while?" Kendra ventured.

Eleanor's dark eyes twinkled with a sort of benevolent mischief. "That would be my guess, from the few conversations I've had with him."

"Why does he want such a big piece of land?" The Macabees' ranch must have been upwards of five hundred acres. It wasn't your usual hobby farm.

Eleanor shrugged. "I didn't ask," she said. "He's a nice man, and soooo good-looking."

Kendra laughed, even though the thought of Gage Elder as a permanent fixture made her distinctly nervous. She supposed on some level, she'd been expecting him to get bored with country life and head back to the bright lights.

It was oddly comforting to know she'd been wrong.

Maybe.

After good-byes and promises to get together for a good visit one of these days soon, Kendra and Eleanor said their farewells and went their separate ways, Eleanor heading for Gage Elder's place and Kendra—well, she'd decided to lock up and make for the cottage/guest house and try to do something constructive.

Which would be a challenge, given that her thoughts were stuck on the rodeo champion/stuntman once more.

If he asked her out again—which he probably wouldn't, given how unreceptive she'd been—perhaps she ought to agree, go out to dinner and see a movie with him.

It wasn't as if he was likely to jump her bones or anything.

He was basically a cowboy, and that might mean he lived by the corresponding code; most of the cowboys she'd known were strong, forthright men who respected women and treated them accordingly.

Then again, that could be an act. Sure, he lived in the country, rode horseback and dressed in jeans and cotton shirts with snaps on the pockets and wore scuffed boots, but that didn't mean he wasn't playing a role.

And what about the woman and the girl she'd seen with him in the diner earlier that day? They didn't live in or around Copper Ridge, Kendra knew that much, but what if they were his wife and daughter?

Should she Google to find out?

Kendra paused, closing the heavy door of the mansion behind her and turning the key in the lock. If Gage was married, or involved, would he have had the brass to bring his family into the diner while she was there, working?

But, then, maybe he hadn't expected her to be there, or simply hadn't thought about the matter in the first place.

Annoyed with herself, Kendra murmured as she descended the steps at the side of the main house and started up the curving stone walkway that led to her cottage.

It was a sweet little place, that cottage, surrounded by blooming roses, irises, gerbera daisies, the works. In fact, it resembled one of the diamond paintings her grandmother used to work on in the evenings.

In the fading light of a summer day, visited by butterflies, that little house seemed to glow.

The sight of it lifted Kendra's spirits.

She'd gone through her yoga routine, taken a shower and put on jean-shorts and tank top when her smartphone rang.

Harper O'Ballivan's name flickered on the screen.

"Hello, Mrs. O'Ballivan," Kendra said, after accepting the call. "What can I do for you on this fine summer evening?"

Harper laughed. She sounded tired, but happy, and little wonder. She and Jack had three kids now, counting Jack's son, Gideon, from an earlier relationship, and she was usually busy with her children or her job as a school guidance counselor.

Of course, since it was summer, and school was out, she didn't have to go to work, at least.

"You can promise to come to the party Jack and I are throwing next weekend, here on the ranch, that's what you can do for me. It'll be big—most of the town will probably be there—and it's going to be lots of fun. Pony rides for the kids. Music and dancing for the grown-ups. And, of course, a barbecue. Say you'll be there!"

Kendra smiled to herself. The O'Ballivans were famous for their ginormous outdoor parties. One time, she'd heard, they'd even had a real carousel brought in and set up.

She'd still been married to Ethan back then, and the goings-on in Copper Ridge were something she rarely thought about.

"Of course I'll come," she told Harper, then hesitated. "But what if I'm scheduled to work at the diner that day?"

"No worries. The Hot-N-Tot will be closed for business between Friday night and Sunday morning."

No one had told Kendra about the plan to close the diner, but that wasn't anything new. The owner, Maggie Alcorn, was even busier than Kendra herself, juggling a young family, commitments to various charities and a bustling diner just off the much-traveled highway leading downstate to Phoenix and beyond.

"Well, I guess that's settled then," Kendra conceded.

She wondered if Jack and Harper had invited Gage Elder to their shindig, decided they probably had, since they liked to include almost everybody in their celebrations, especially if they were new in town.

She wasn't about to ask.

"Good," Harper said.

"What's the dress code?"

Again, Harper laughed. She sounded so *happy*. Clearly, her marriage and family brought her a lot of joy.

What would that feel like? Kendra wondered. To be genuinely loved by a good man, a man she could trust? One who would take her side if she was being hassled?

And to have his children—

To finally be a mother.

Stop it, she told herself silently.

"The dress code?" Harper echoed. "There isn't one. You can come in jeans and a T-shirt, a sundress, a fancy ball gown—whatever. Just be there."

"What are *you* wearing?" Kendra pressed, with a smile.

"Jeans, a blouse and boots," Harper answered. "Jack's going to saddle up some horses and lead whoever wants to go on a trail ride up into the hills. The view from there is staggeringly beautiful, especially at sunset."

"Sounds good," Kendra said, imagining the panorama of Arizona countryside from up in the hills bordering the O'Ballivan ranch.

When was the last time she'd ridden a horse?

She couldn't remember, but she was open to the idea.

Pretty much.

Chapter 3

A party.

Well, Gage hadn't been expecting that.

After leaving the diner and saying good-bye to his sister and niece, he'd driven straight home, changed his clothes and whistled for his horse, Max, who seemed reluctant to obey the summons, preferring to graze in the pasture at his leisure.

Gage had been thinking a ride in the fresh air and fading shimmer of the day might clear his head—he couldn't quite shake the image of Kendra, back there at the diner, trying to pretend she didn't want to drop everything and head for the hills rather than interact with him—but then he remembered his appointment with Eleanor Hartford, the real estate agent he'd originally contacted about buying the Macabee place.

The ride would have to wait.

He was carrying the saddle back into the small, ramshackle barn when a truck pulled in, big and shiny and black, with a reinforced grill.

Gage recognized the rig, and the driver, immediately.

It was Jack O'Ballivan, one of his neighbors. He'd known

Jack long before either of them had settled near Copper Ridge, as they'd been investors in some of the same start-ups.

Gage stopped in the yard, a rocky space between the barn and his double-wide trailer, greeted his friend with a grin and a brief wave of his hand.

Stanley, delighted at the prospect of company, as always, was barking his head off, hysterical with joy.

Jack parked the truck, waited a few seconds for the inevitable dust to settle, and got out of the rig. He laughed as Stanley ran to greet him, bending to ruffle the critter's ears affectionately.

"Hey," Gage said, that being his standard greeting when it came to his male friends.

Jack, a tall man with dark hair and piercing blue eyes, ambled toward him, smiling. "Hey," he replied, putting out a hand.

"To what do I owe the honor?" Gage asked, as they shook.

Seeing Jack cheered him up a little. After all, the ranch was a lonely place, especially now that Sophie and Brittany had gone back to Phoenix following a four-day visit.

Maybe it was a mistake, adding five hundred acres to the property, but his gut instinct said go ahead, so he meant to.

Jack was still smiling. "The wife sent me to remind you that we're holding a get-together this Saturday over at our place, starting around noon. It'll be quite a dust-up—dancing, horseback riding, a barbecue with all the trimmings. You'll join us, I hope?"

Inwardly, Gage sighed.

He'd become something of an introvert since Summer's death, and big shindigs like the one the O'Ballivans were throwing tended to make him withdraw further into himself instead of drawing him out. For that reason, he usually countered by wading in and making the best of whatever situation he encountered.

If he allowed himself to retreat, he figured, he'd probably turn into a recluse, stewing in his own shortcomings.

Not gonna happen, he thought.

"Sure," he told Jack. "I'll be there. Anything I can do to help with the setup?"

"Good," Jack responded, nodding. "I'll be heading up a trail ride. Maybe you could saddle that gelding of yours and ride over to our place instead of driving. We can always use another cowboy on the trail ride."

"I'll do that," Gage replied, happy with the plan. He was always more comfortable in the saddle than anywhere else. Just about anywhere else, anyway. "Max could do with some exposure to other horses anyhow. He's a little skittish."

Jack was nodding again when a bright red Escalade turned in at the open gate and rolled up the driveway toward them.

Eleanor had arrived, right on schedule.

Jack, familiar with the woman, like most everybody within a fifty-mile radius, smiled and waved toward her.

She gave the horn a couple of cheery toots, pulled up beside Jack's truck, and got out before either of the two men could help her.

Eleanor was independent, that was for sure.

Her smile was broad as she greeted them.

"This must be my lucky day," she joked. "Two handsome cowboys, all to myself."

Both Jack and Gage chuckled at the remark.

Stanley, meanwhile, wrapped his dusty self around Eleanor's legs and wove a figure eight.

With a generous laugh, she acknowledged the dog with a pat on the head.

"We're the lucky ones," Jack responded, before Gage could say anything. "Did Harper send you an email about the party this Saturday?"

"Yes, she did," Eleanor replied. "I read it on my phone back at the railroad crossing between here and town. That was one long-ass train."

Both men laughed.

"And you said yes?" Jack prompted.

"I sure did," Eleanor answered.

With that, Jack ended his visit, shaking Gage's hand again, giving Eleanor a polite hug.

Once he'd jumped back into his truck and driven away, Gage gestured for Eleanor to precede him into the double-wide. She pressed a palm to her forehead and said she'd left her briefcase in the back seat of her car; she'd fetch it and be right with him.

Gage retrieved the leather case instead and brought it back to her.

She thanked him, and they climbed the steps onto the small deck, then went inside, ending up in the spacious living room, with its skylights and built-in bookshelves.

Stanley approached the couch, cast a questioning glance at Gage, then gave a dog-sigh and crossed to his well-padded bed over by the gas-powered fireplace.

Eleanor looked around, clearly appreciating the design of the place. "I guess I forgot since last time I was here just how beautiful this place is," she said.

"Thanks," Gage muttered, somewhat at a loss. He was shy, though he didn't like admitting that, even to himself. "Please—have a seat." He gestured toward a big, cushy armchair near the matching couch. "Can I get you anything? Coffee? Water?"

Still smiling, Eleanor sat down in the armchair. "Water would be nice. Thank you."

Gage fetched a bottle from the Sub-Zero fridge in the well-appointed kitchen, returned to the living room and handed it over.

Stanley had settled down in his dog bed, and he was already snoring.

Gage took a seat on the end of the couch nearest Eleanor's chair and interlaced his fingers. "So," he ventured, suddenly nervous. "What did the Macabees say to my offer?"

Eleanor's face shone like a beacon in a lighthouse. "They accepted it, with pleasure," she said, opening her briefcase and extracting a small cluster of documents. "They've agreed to close on the property within the month."

Gage heaved a sigh of relief. He hadn't realized, until then, how anxious he was for this deal to go through. "Good," he said.

"There is one stipulation," Eleanor interjected.

Gage tensed slightly. There would be a problem if the Macabees wanted their original house and barn to remain; he planned to have those bulldozed as soon as the ink dried on the contracts.

"There's a private cemetery on the property," Eleanor went on. "It's on a hilltop, in a copse of trees, and the Macabees have been burying their dead there since the late eighteen hundreds. They're asking that you leave that particular part of the ranch as is, and permit them to visit from time to time. They'll ask for your permission first, of course."

Gage was relieved. Again. "No problem," he said. "I'll fence the place in, to protect it from stray cattle and wild horses, and the Macabees and their kin are welcome there anytime—no advance notice needed."

Eleanor glowed again, leaned over to pat Gage's upper arm in appreciation. "Thank you," she said. "That will mean a lot to those folks."

After that, she laid a small stack of documents on the coffee table and handed Gage a gleaming pen with her business name and logo on the side.

Gage signed, and signed again, while Eleanor sipped from her water bottle and looked around the room, taking in the art collection and the framed photos on one long wall.

Eventually, she got to her feet and approached the photos, taking them in.

Finished signing papers, Gage went to join her.

Eleanor took in the celebrity photos, but her main interest seemed to be focused on pictures of Gage and Sophie as children and teenagers, then the portrait of Summer, standing on a beach, rimmed by a halo of sunlight, slender and strong and pensive as she gazed at something far off in the distance.

Gage's throat tightened as it always did when he looked at that photo.

She'd been so beautiful, Summer had. So kind and so very smart.

And he'd loved her desperately.

In fact, he still did, though in a quieter, softer way than before.

What he'd said to Brittany earlier that day, at the diner, was true. He would never get over Summer.

So why was he so attracted to Kendra Spencer?

"Your wife?" Eleanor asked gently, cautiously, touching the frame of Summer's portrait with the tip of one index finger.

"Yes," Gage answered, marveling, not for the first time, at the singular communication network of a small town. As the old cliché went, word got around. "Her name was Summer. She died in an accident six years ago."

"I'm so sorry," Eleanor said softly.

"It was hard, losing her," Gage heard himself say, and the sound of his own voice caught him off guard, because he hadn't planned on discussing Summer's passing.

"Of course it was." The tender caring in Eleanor's tone brought tears to the back of Gage's eyes, and they stung like all get-out. It was a fight not to turn them loose. "Did you have any children?"

Gage, careful not to look at Eleanor, kept his gaze on Summer's image. His right hand moved slightly, as if to rise and brush aside the blonde strands floating across her forehead, but he stopped the motion immediately.

"No kids," he responded, sounding gruff now. Sad.

Eleanor didn't seem to know what to say to that, as she didn't speak right away.

Meanwhile, Gage pulled himself together. Stiffened his spine a little and returned his shoulders to their usual squared setting.

"I guess I shouldn't have asked," Eleanor said, with a regretful sigh.

At that, Gage turned to face the woman.

He liked her a lot, and he didn't want her feeling guilty over a perfectly natural question.

"It's okay," he told her. "It's been six years."

Eleanor's face brightened, but her dark eyes reflected the sorrow Gage felt whenever he thought of his late wife, the children they'd wanted and never had, the adventures they might have shared, all of it.

"I lost my first husband twenty years ago," she said, "and I miss him to this very day."

She lifted her left hand to smooth a lock of hair back from her cheek, and Gage's gaze caught on her wide gold wedding band.

He didn't ask, but she must have seen the question in his eyes, for she answered it.

"I remarried a few years back," she confided, "and I love my present husband, Clyde, every bit as deeply as I loved Fred, my first one. Time was, I thought I'd never be able to move on—losing Fred nearly destroyed me—but then I met Clyde at a church social—he'd just moved to Copper Ridge from up in Montana and I liked him right away. We talked about stuff like our shared interest in gardening, took walks together, simple things like that. And gradually that liking turned to love."

There, Eleanor paused, her cheeks brightening.

"There I go," she went on, after a few moments of fretful silence, "running my mouth again. Sometimes I get to yammering and I just can't stop myself."

Gage wasn't bothered. The things Eleanor had said had lodged in the darkest part of his heart, breaking down walls, letting in the light.

They turned from the wall of photos, and a calm silence fell.

Eleanor gathered up the signed documents, tucked them briskly back into her briefcase, and put out her hand. "Welcome to Copper Ridge, Gage Elder," she said. "I'm just about positive you belong here."

For the first time since he'd settled in the area, Gage felt as though he really *did* belong in this place.

He opened the front door for Eleanor and then walked her back to her Escalade. Lent a hand as she climbed into the driver's seat.

"I guess I'll see you at the party on Saturday," Gage said, because he needed to say *something* and that was all that came to mind.

"You surely will," Eleanor said, with another of her high-octane smiles. "I've got to warn you ahead of time, though. You're going to have to fight off a whole slew of women. You're a hot topic around town, Mr. Elder."

Gage shook his head. Smiled. He wasn't interested in a "whole slew" of women.

Only in one.

Would Kendra be at the get-together?

He heard himself ask that question aloud, and hoped the stubble on his chin and cheeks hid the rush of color he felt surging toward the surface like a flood-tide.

Eleanor, still smiling, arched an eyebrow. "I'm sure she will," she replied. "She and Harper O'Ballivan, Jack's wife, are good friends."

Gage rubbed the side of his face with one hand, hoping to

quell the blush pounding there. He didn't know what to say without getting himself in deeper, so he kept silent.

Eleanor pulled the car door shut, rolled down the window, started the engine. "Thanks again, and I'll see you on Saturday."

Gage could only nod.

Behind the embarrassment, he was still going over what Eleanor had said about loving her first husband, who was long gone, and caring just as much for her new spouse.

Was that possible—loving two people at once?

Was that a form of cheating, at least on an emotional level?

Confused, he sighed and shoved a hand through his hair.

Then he headed for the pasture fence and whistled for Max again.

This time, the gelding came trotting toward him, nickering a greeting and tossing his head.

"Brace yourself, buddy," Gage told the animal. "We're going for a ride."

Chapter 4

Three days until the community gathering at the O'Ballivans' ranch.

Kendra had been thinking about the event—when she wasn't ruminating over Gage Elder or what to do with Spencer House—ever since Harper had invited her to attend.

And she was still mulling it over early that fateful Tuesday morning, when she opened the diner for business, an hour or so ahead of the usual breakfast rush.

Mike Drummond, the cook, was running late that morning, according to the message he'd texted Kendra, but he promised to be there as soon as possible.

That meant she was alone in the diner, but that was kind of nice.

It gave her time, if only a few minutes, most likely, to prepare herself for the day ahead.

On impulse, she popped a few quarters into the vintage jukebox in a corner of the room, chose some old-fashioned country favorites, and stepped behind the counter to fire up the big steel coffee maker.

She was measuring grounds into the machine dedicated to decaf and humming along with Emmylou Harris's "One of These Days" when she heard the main door open and felt a rush of cool air.

She turned, smiling, expecting to see Mike, the cook.

Instead, she saw Gage Elder standing there, looking somewhat sheepish.

And damnably handsome in his cowboy getup of jeans, a cotton shirt and denim jacket, and boots.

"Umm—the OPEN sign is on," he ventured, sounding as uncomfortable as Kendra felt. "I thought—"

She nodded. She'd flipped the switch on her way in, lighting up the neon sign in the front window.

After a few deep breaths, surprisingly, most if not all of Kendra's reservations about this man receded.

She maintained the smile she'd meant for Mike.

"It's okay, Mr. Elder," she said. "We're open. Come on in and have a seat. The cook isn't here yet, but I'll do my best to fill your order."

Did she just say that? She, Kendra Spencer, who feared all men? Especially the attractive ones, like Gage Elder?

Kendra blushed a little, but she still felt strangely bold.

"Gage, please," he corrected. He looked as nervous as she usually felt whenever she encountered him, but he walked across the vinyl-tiled floor of the diner and took a seat at the counter.

"Gage, then," she conceded pleasantly. "I'm Kendra."

"I know," Gage replied. Then he ran one hand over his face and squared his shoulders. "I mean, this is a small town and everything—"

Strangely, Kendra wanted to laugh.

Instead, she asked, "Coffee? Cream and sugar?"

Gage nodded, still looking mildly flustered. He clearly hadn't expected to run into Kendra that morning any more than she'd expected to run into him.

"Yeah, coffee, please," he said. "Black."

Kendra grabbed a clean mug, stepped in front of the coffee machine, and lowered the lever. "It's fresh," she told him, turning to set the steaming mug before him on the countertop. "Just brewed."

"Thanks," he said. He'd been avoiding her gaze so far—or, at least, that was the impression Kendra had gotten—but now their gazes met, in a silent and slightly electrified collision.

Kendra felt her heart skip a beat, though she was able to keep her cool.

She hoped.

"The breakfast special is sausage hash with eggs and toast," she said. It was like listening to someone else speak, rather than herself.

That was when Gage grinned, and that, coupled with the light of easy amusement in his blue-green eyes, nearly knocked Kendra back on her heels. With a shake of his head, he replied, "No breakfast for me. I'll have something later, when I get home."

Kendra wanted to ask where he'd been, so early in the morning, if breakfast hadn't been a factor but, of course, she didn't. So much for her initial calmness; now she felt like a woman dancing atop a rolling log while roaring floodwaters carried her toward Niagara Falls.

"You're in town early," she observed, after much consideration.

The conversation was awkward, but silence would be even more so.

"I'm supposed to pick up a litter of puppies—part of a litter, anyway—from a guy who lives over on the other side of town. It'll be a while before I can knock on his door, but I couldn't sleep for worrying about those little dogs, so I fed my horse and the dog I already have and drove in from my place."

"You're adopting puppies?"

"There are only three. I'm planning to foster them until I can find them good homes."

Now he'd *really* caught Kendra's attention.

She'd been wanting a dog for a long time.

Maybe this was a sign from heaven.

"Could I see them? The puppies I mean?"

Gage seemed pleased. "Sure. I can bring them by the diner later, if you like—or bring them by your place—" At this, he shifted from delighted to uncertain. "I mean, if that would be okay."

She hesitated to commit to a location—at least, not yet—but Gage wasn't amenable to waiting around, evidently, because he immediately added, "I think you and I got off on the wrong foot, Kendra. If I did or said anything to make you feel uncomfortable, I'm truly sorry."

Kendra was just about to reply that he hadn't made her uncomfortable, which would have been a lie, when the unbelievable happened.

The diner door swung open, and *he* stepped inside.

Ethan Larkin was standing right there, before her eyes.

He looked thinner, almost gaunt, in fact, and his dark hair was graying at the temples.

He smiled as though he expected a joyful welcome. And maybe he did, narcissist that he was.

"Hello, Kendra," he said.

Kendra opened her mouth, closed it again.

"Should I leave?" Gage asked her, very quietly. He must have turned to see who had walked in when he saw Kendra's reaction to the new arrival, because he was facing Ethan now.

She found her voice, enough of it, anyway, to whisper, "*No. Please stay.*"

"You got it," Gage answered. His expression was grim as he surveyed the man who had startled her so badly.

"What are you doing here, Ethan?" she finally managed to ask. With Gage beside her, she felt stronger, better able to cope with the shock.

"I thought you would have read about it on social media," Ethan answered amiably. Did he *really* think she was glad to see him? Incredible. "Let me tell you, it was a shitstorm, but I've seen the error of my ways. Severed ties with Desuma and Elyse—for good. I'm here to start over with you."

Kendra made her way to the nearest table and sank into a chair.

Gage followed; she sensed that he was standing right behind her.

Ethan took a step in her direction, looked past her to Gage, and stopped where he was.

"You can't be serious," Kendra said, her temper rising. "You can't really think I would take you back, after all that happened?"

Ethan shrugged, looking affable and, damn it, unfazed. "Okay, so maybe it will take some time to win you over. That's why I signed up for a stay at the Sunset Motel." He paused, shuddered slightly. "It's a tacky joint, but I couldn't find anything else on short notice."

"Where's Walter?" Kendra asked, though she hadn't planned to. Hadn't even thought of the dog, as much as she'd loved him.

"He's outside, in the back seat of my car," Ethan replied, still blithely confident. "Want to see him?"

Of course she wanted to see Walter, but for now, she chose not to.

A reunion with that sweet animal would only make saying good-bye to him again harder than it had been the first time.

Kendra merely shook her head. She felt dizzy, light-headed.

The diner floor seemed to tilt slightly, then right itself with a wallop.

On the jukebox, Patsy Cline's "Crazy" kicked in.

She'd been crazy, all right, Kendra thought. Crazy for loving Ethan.

Just when she thought she might topple to one side out of sheer overwhelm, Kendra felt Gage's hand come to rest on her shoulder.

It was as though his strength was flowing into her, and she immediately sat up straight again.

"I don't think we've met," Ethan said, looking past Kendra to Gage. He sounded anything but friendly, despite the way he'd been behaving.

Gage squeezed Kendra's shoulder gently. Reassuringly. "Nope," he replied simply. "Our paths have never crossed."

"Ethan Larkin," Ethan said, all cheery again, though the ice in his eyes hadn't melted. "I'm Kendra's first love."

"My ex-husband," Kendra clarified.

"Gage Elder," Gage said, but he made no move to leave his post behind Kendra's chair or put out a hand to Ethan for a gentlemanly shake.

Ethan nodded, but when the door opened behind him, admitting Mike, he seemed ready to back off a little.

Ethan liked to present himself well, at least in public.

"You know where to reach me," he told Kendra.

And then he left.

Mike, apparently oblivious to the drama, scuffled on into the kitchen to heat up the grill. Cars were already pulling into the parking lot across from the diner, their headlights streaking by the windows like golden ghosts on the fly.

Gage pulled up a chair next to Kendra and sat down. "Are you all right?" he asked, and he sounded genuinely concerned.

"No," Kendra answered, with an awkward attempt at a

laugh. "I was counting on never seeing that man again. I should have known fate would throw a wrench in the works."

Gage offered a slight smile, an upward tilt of one side of his mouth.

He hadn't shaved, Kendra noted, apropos of nothing.

Nothing except the desire to caress his face with both hands and thank him for being so supportive when Ethan appeared, that is.

"I could stick around for a while—"

Kendra shook her head, smiled. "No, that's okay. Mike's here now, and within the next five minutes, the place will be full. I'm safe, Gage. Really."

He touched her hand, and yet another jolt of electricity zipped through her.

"If you say so," he said. "Still want to see the pups later on?"

Kendra nodded. "Yes," she answered.

"Then how about stopping by my place after you get off work? I'll have them all settled in by then." He paused. "And I promise you'll be safe with me, Kendra."

Now that she'd seen Gage stand up for her, Kendra believed him.

So many men would have left when Ethan showed up, thinking they'd be in the way if they stayed.

Gage Elder had waited to see if he'd be needed.

To her surprise, after Gage got to his feet, he bent and placed a light kiss on her forehead. "I'll settle up for the coffee now and be on my way," he said.

"No charge for the coffee," Kendra said, all shivery inside. "It's on me."

This time, it wasn't fear that moved her. "I'll see you around two thirty this afternoon," she added. "You live on the place with the nice double-wide trailer, just down the road from the O'Ballivan place, right?"

He smiled. "Right," he replied. "See you then."

With that, he was on his way out.

Kendra felt a strange ache, seeing him leave, and the encounter with Ethan had left her anxious and unnerved.

She also felt the beginning of a headache thumping at the base of her skull, but she ignored it, out of necessity.

Customers were practically pouring into the diner by then, smiling at Kendra, calling out jovial hellos to Mike, back there in the kitchen, ready for a busy day.

Kendra threw herself wholeheartedly into the job, greeting everyone, bringing them coffee or orange juice, along with menus.

Around nine a.m., Beth Robbins, the other waitress assigned to the early shift, rushed in, tying her apron strings behind her as she came.

"I'm sorry," she blurted, passing Kendra, who was carrying plates of pancakes, bacon, and eggs. "I'm sorry, I'm sorry, I'm sorry."

Kendra chuckled. "Chill out, Beth. I've managed to handle everything so far." *Yeah, everything*, taunted a voice inside Kendra's mind. *You handled a ridiculous attraction to Gage Elder and a face-to-face confrontation with your ex-husband, who evidently wants to pretend that you're crazy about him.* "Make the rounds with the coffeepot—don't forget the decaf—after that, we'll split the floor fifty-fifty like we usually do."

Beth, a pretty nineteen-year-old recently married to her high school sweetheart, Jason, still looked flustered. "Okay," she said, still sounding breathless. "Roger that."

Kendra chuckled again.

And then went about her business, as did Beth.

When quitting time finally rolled around, hours later, Kendra's feet were aching, as usual, and it was harder to keep thoughts of Ethan at bay.

Why in the *world* had he come looking for her, when he'd

had no shortage of women at his beck and call, probably even while he and Kendra were still married?

What reason could he possibly have for showing up out of nowhere the way he had, and acting as if he expected her to fall at his feet in pure gratitude?

It was a mystery to Kendra, but she managed to shake it off pretty quickly.

Her attention was focused on Gage Elder, and the puppies he was fostering.

She hadn't even asked what breed they were.

Probably mixed, rather than purebred.

Not that it mattered to Kendra.

Training a puppy would be a hassle for sure, but that didn't bother her, either. She knew, with a dog to keep her company, that she wouldn't be as lonely as she had been up to now.

In any case, she was pretty sure she'd be bringing one of them home that day.

She wanted to head straight for Gage's place, but she made herself slow down and concentrate on preparations. She changed out of her uniform, donning jeans and a tank top, and drove to the pet shop for supplies—a cushy little bed, a few toys, the food recommended for puppies.

With all those things tucked into the back seat, Kendra drove out of town, full of hope—and worry over Ethan's sudden reappearance in her life.

That last part could wait, though.

For now, she was going to see a litter of three puppies.

And spend a little time with Gage Elder.

that no [illegible] or woman in his bed, and will probably even while he and Kendra were still married?

What [illegible] could he possibly [illegible] up on [illegible] there [illegible] and [illegible] as if he [illegible] all his [illegible] gratitude?

It was [illegible] to Kendra, but she [illegible] pretty [illegible]

[illegible] enough [illegible] Cape Cod [illegible] and [illegible] listening.

She hadn't even asked [illegible]

Probably [illegible]

Not that it mattered to Kendra.

[illegible] would be a hassle [illegible] but that didn't bother her [illegible]. She knew [illegible] to keep her company, [illegible] as she had been up to now.

In any case, she was pretty sure she'd be [illegible] than [illegible] that day.

She [illegible] but she [illegible] without [illegible] she [illegible] out of [illegible] and [illegible] the [illegible] a few days, the [illegible] as [illegible]

With all those things tucked into the back seat, Kendra [illegible], over [illegible] and [illegible] in her [illegible]

Then [illegible] could [illegible] all.

For [illegible] she was going [illegible] pumps [illegible]

[illegible] Cape Cod.

Chapter 5

Stanley barked with his usual enthusiasm as Kendra pulled in, driving her ordinary blue sedan.

Gage, busy with the puppies until then, stepped out onto the small, simple deck to greet her.

She parked her car a short distance from the trailer, pushed open the door and got out, smiling a smile that sent a thrill zipping through his midsection and straight up his spine.

He whistled for Stanley to back off—his enthusiasm over Kendra's arrival had the volition of a steamroller in high gear—and, reluctantly, the dog turned and trotted back to the steps of the deck, where Gage waited. He had one of the fostered pups—a little brown and white fluffball of a guy he suspected he would end up keeping for good—squirming in the curve of his left arm.

Kendra, who had seemed delighted by Stanley's approach, lit up when she spotted the pup, and quickened her steps.

"He's so cute!" she enthused, reaching out for the tiny dog with eager hands.

"What breed is he?"

"Part Shih Tzu, I think, with some poodle mixed in," Gage answered, grinning as the puppy stretched himself to lick Kendra's cheek.

Gage stepped back, gestured toward the open door, leading into the front room. The other two pups were curled up together on a thick, folded blanket resting in a corner.

One was black and white, the other mostly black.

Kendra seemed magnetized to the tiny critters, handing the pup she'd been holding to Gage, crossing the length of the room and kneeling next to the other two puppies.

Watching Kendra take such a tender interest in these animals, who had basically been discarded like so much trash, did something to Gage. Something profound and totally indescribable.

She looked back at him over one shoulder, her eyes bright with tears. "They weren't wanted," she said. It wasn't quite a question, since she knew Gage had picked them up at someone's house, intending to rehome them at some point.

Saddened, because she was saddened, Gage shook his head. "Fletch Wilkins isn't the kindest man on the face of the earth. Evidently, his daughter's dog bred with a stray, and these three were the result."

He reached past Kendra, who was still kneeling, to put the brown and white puppy back on the improvised bed with his brothers.

"Why didn't he take them to the shelter?" she pressed.

Gage shook his head. "I don't know. Too much trouble, I suspect. I heard Fletch talking to a friend of his in the hardware store a few days ago, and he said he had some mutts to get rid of, pronto. I was afraid he meant to shoot the poor critters, or toss them into the creek, so I interrupted the conversation and offered the old man some cash for the dogs. He agreed, said he'd have to speak with his daughter before he could say for sure, but he took the money. After a day or two, he called to say I could pick them up this morning. So I did."

By then, Kendra was holding the black-and-white pup close against her chest, and tears slipped down her cheeks.

She sniffled, then rose to her feet, still holding the black and white. "I'd like this one, please," she told Gage. "I'm willing to pay for him, of course—"

"No need of that," Gage thought, aware that his voice had turned gruff all of a sudden. "I know you'll give him a good home, and that's all I care about."

Kendra kissed the top of the dog's head, still cuddling him close. "Thank you," she said, with another sniffle. "I'm already madly in love with him—his name, as of this moment, is Oreo."

Gage laughed at that. "Excellent," he said. "It fits."

Kendra nodded, buried her face in Oreo's thick fur for a moment.

Stanley had joined them at some point, and he was standing beside the dog bed, rather like a guard. Gage had pretty much decided to keep one of the two remaining pups; now, he figured he'd wind up keeping both of them.

He said as much, while opening a cupboard and taking out two tall glasses, filling them with ice at the refrigerator, then grabbing two cans of sparkling water from inside.

"Stay a while?" he asked.

Kendra hesitated for a moment, but then she sat down on one of the benches at the long trestle table. Accepted the offer of cold, fizzy water with a murmured "thanks," the puppy settled in her lap by then.

For a minute or so, both Kendra and Gage remained silent.

Then, after a few restorative sips of ice water, Gage spoke. "So," he began thoughtfully, carefully, lest she panic and bolt, "that guy who showed up at the diner this morning. Ethan, wasn't it?"

Kendra sighed, averted her gaze for a moment or so, then met Gage's eyes.

"Yes. Ethan Larkin. He's my ex-husband."

"Yeah, I remember. Is he dangerous or something? You seemed pretty rattled when he walked in."

Kendra bit her lower lip, swallowed visibly, even though she hadn't lifted her glass from the tabletop again.

Then she shook her head. "I don't think Ethan would hurt me physically," she replied. "It's just—well, things ended really badly between he and I. Some relatives of his fed him some nasty lies about me—that I'd been cheating with a colleague from work—and he believed them. I tried reasoning with him, but he refused to listen. On top of losing my baby, that was too much. We ended up divorcing—we lived up in Seattle at the time—and I came home to Copper Ridge a few weeks later."

Gage let out a long breath. "That's rough," he said. Then, with an effort at a smile, "You grew up here in town?"

"I did," Kendra confirmed, cheering up a little, maybe because of the puppy squirming in her lap. "My grandmother raised me in Spencer House. When she passed, I inherited the place, though I live in the cottage out back. The mansion is too big for one woman"—she paused, kissed the top of Oreo's head again—"and now, one dog."

"Do you like working at the diner?"

She shrugged. "It's okay. Gets me out of the house. I tend to isolate myself too much if I stay home a lot."

Gage spread his hands slightly. "Your turn to ask a question," he said, with a slight smile.

Kendra smiled back, though her eyes were still misted with the aftermath of her tears. "Fair enough," she said. Then she drew a very deep breath and let it out slowly. "Okay, here goes. Are you married?"

Gage was taken aback, just a little. "Me?" he asked. "No. I'm a widower."

Her eyes widened in sympathy. "I'm so sorry."

"It's been a while," he allowed quietly.

"Do you have a girlfriend, then?" she asked, blushing a bit.

The pieces were falling into place then—she'd seen him with Sophie and Brittany that day, at the diner, and probably had no clue who they were. Gage wanted to laugh, but he knew that would be a mistake, given the fact that the two of them were on shaky emotional ground.

The situation was delicate, and he didn't want to blow his chance to get to know this woman.

"No," Gage said, "I'm not involved with anyone at the moment. The two ladies you saw me with at the Hot N Tot were my sister, Sophie, and my niece, Brittany. They live in Phoenix and drove up to spend a few days with me."

Kendra's cheeks were a little pinker than before. "Oh," she said.

Gage grinned. "You didn't really think I was the kind of guy who'd ask a woman out when I already had a wife or a girlfriend?"

"No," Kendra answered, after a few moments of contemplation. "I admit the possibility crossed my mind, though. I haven't had the best experience with men, and besides, you're a celebrity."

"I'm *not* a celebrity," Gage countered, but pleasantly. "I was a stuntman, yes, and I've won a few buckles in a few rodeos, but that doesn't mean I'm famous."

Kendra laughed, though she still sounded a bit nervous. "Au contraire," she replied. "In Copper Ridge, you're a star."

"That's ridiculous," Gage objected.

"Maybe so," Kendra retorted cheerfully, "but it's true."

"Crap," Gage said.

"You're going to the party at the O'Ballivans' place on Saturday, right?"

"Yeah," he replied, without much enthusiasm, remembering what Eleanor Hartford, the Realtor, had said about "a whole slew of women" being after him. "I'm starting to think I ought to skip it, though."

"You're *shy*," Kendra pointed out, apparently delighted by the discovery.

Gage's face felt warm beneath the stubble on his chin. He'd known Kendra was going to show up to take a look at the pups. Why hadn't he shaved?

"Maybe I am," he agreed.

"You can't miss the party, Gage. Harper and Jack will be disappointed if you do."

"I don't imagine they'd miss me, considering that they invited practically everybody in the county," Gage argued.

"I dare you to go," Kendra said. For the next few moments, she looked as if she'd embarrassed herself a little by being so straightforward.

"Okay, I'll go. On one condition."

She arched one eyebrow. "What condition?"

"You and I go together. We'll call it a date."

Kendra leaned back a little, then straightened her spine. "Well—I—"

"Now who's being shy?" Gage challenged, amused. Hopeful.

She hesitated.

"Kendra," he added, more serious now, "I'm not your ex. I'm a whole different kind of man, and I think you know that."

She let out a breath of concession. "All right," she said. "It's a date." A pause followed. "And nothing more."

Gage grinned. "Agreed," he said. "I promised to help Jack with a trail ride, so I need to get there around noon or so. I'll pick you up at your place at eleven thirty, if that works for you."

Kendra looked both nervous and eager, which was a fascinating puzzle, one Gage was happy to solve.

"I guess I could help Harper with the preparations while you're working with Jack. There will probably be a lot of things to do, even though some big restaurant up in Flagstaff is catering the whole event."

"Or," Gage replied lightly, "you could join us on the trail ride."

"I haven't ridden a horse since before I left for college," Kendra objected, still holding the puppy, who had fallen back to sleep.

"You're scared of horses?" Gage asked, but gently, and with good humor.

"I *love* horses," she answered. "It's just that I'm out of practice."

"Then I guess Saturday would be a good time to get back in the game."

Once again, Kendra raised an eyebrow. "You're being pretty persistent," she remarked.

"I guess I am," Gage agreed. "But, to use your own words, I dare you."

She narrowed her eyes, but the corners of her mouth—her very kissable mouth—twitched a little. "If I get thrown and break my neck, Gage Elder, it will be your fault."

He laughed. "That isn't going to happen. I'm pretty sure Jack O'Ballivan can come up with a sway-backed nag that moves at the speed of a plow horse."

Kendra struggled visibly not to smile, but she lost the battle. "Okay, you win. *This time.* I'll see you at eleven thirty on Saturday." With that, she stood up, Oreo safe in her arms. "In the meantime, I'd better get home and get this little fella all settled in."

Gage rose, walked her toward the front door.

She looked around as he opened it for her. "This place is really nice," she said.

"It'll do for now," Gage replied, as they went outside.

"You don't plan on living here permanently?" she asked, taking the deck steps carefully.

"I'm buying the Macabee ranch," he said. "Once I've figured out just how I want everything, I might build a bigger house." He lowered his eyes for a moment. "You know, in case I remarry sometime, and father some kids."

When Gage looked up, she was studying him closely.

"You're a lot braver than I am," she told him. "I've always wanted a family, but I couldn't go through another divorce—or another miscarriage."

It made Gage ache inside, thinking of how badly she'd been hurt.

But, then, he had his issues, too. She couldn't go through another divorce, and he couldn't go through another tragedy like losing Summer in a truly awful car crash.

Life was definitely risky.

"Thanks again," she said, when he didn't comment.

"You're welcome." He accompanied her as far as the car, opened the driver's side door and waited as she leaned in to set Oreo in the back seat, where he immediately began to whimper and fret.

"Maybe I should have bought one of those metal kennel things back at the pet shop," she commented, looking a little sad. "It's just that they're—well, they're *cages.*"

"It isn't far to town," he answered. "Oreo will be fine in the back seat if you go straight home."

Kendra nodded, sighed and got into her car.

She snapped on her seat belt, smiled at Gage and pressed the start button on the dashboard as he closed the car door for her.

He watched as she drove away, wishing she'd stayed longer.

For supper, maybe, and a movie on the big-screen TV in the living room afterward.

"Rein it in, cowboy," he muttered to himself. "One thing at a time."

Stanley stood behind him, giving a low whine.

Gage smiled, patted the dog's head. "Don't be sad, buddy," he told his faithful companion. "We haven't seen the last of Kendra Spencer—or of Oreo."

As he turned, heading back to the double-wide, Stanley frolicked beside him, evidently reassured.

Chapter 6

Back home, Kendra set Oreo down on the patch of lawn between Spencer House and the cottage, waiting as he sniffed the grass here and then there, and finally stopped by a fence post to squat and spray. When finished, he pranced around the yard in a comically regal manner, as though taking pride in the fact that he'd just laid claim to the entire property.

Smiling, Kendra led the way to the cottage's front door, urging him to follow with soft words and clicks of her tongue, used the key and opened it. Oreo trotted happily inside, nose raised, sniffing again.

When they reached the small kitchen, Oreo spotted his dog bed right away, and headed straight for it, settling in comfortably.

Amused and completely, permanently smitten, Kendra was scooping kibble from the bag into his food bowl when a knock sounded at the front door.

Because she was expecting Mrs. Earlman, her neighbor from across the street, who stopped by almost every evening to gossip and share baked goods, and with her hands full setting Oreo's supper down on the floor and then turning to the sink to fill his water bowl, she called out, "It's open! Come on through to the kitchen."

She was as shocked as if she'd just been jabbed with a cattle prod when Ethan appeared, Walter at his side.

For a moment or two, she couldn't speak.

Ethan raised both hands, palms out. "Hey, don't panic, okay? I'm not here to cause trouble." He paused, sighed heavily, and shook his head. "But you need to listen to me, Kendra. That's all I'm asking."

Shaken, Kendra groped for a chair, pulled it back from the table, and sank into it.

"'Don't panic'?" she echoed. "Ethan, you just come waltzing into my house as though everything was okay between us and tell me not to panic?"

Ethan kept his distance, but he didn't retreat.

The scene was like a repeat of that morning's encounter in the diner, and Kendra was overwhelmed.

The dog, Walter, seemed unfazed by the drama pulsing through the room like an electrical charge. He hurried to Kendra, put his large paws on her thighs, and began to lick her face.

Kendra hugged him, careful not to squeeze too hard.

Tears burned in her eyes, and, for the merest fraction of a moment, she almost forgot about Ethan, she was so happy to see that dog.

Oreo, meanwhile, puppy-toddled over to examine the canine newcomer and sniff cautiously at his hind legs.

"Cute dog," Ethan commented.

Again, the anger surged. "*Ethan*," Kendra retorted. "Stop pretending there is anything normal about this situation. *You walked into my house as though you have a right to be here!*"

At this, Ethan rolled his eyes, and Kendra caught a glimpse of something resembling despair in their usually lively depths, something she couldn't quite ignore. "I knocked. You called out to me to come in," he argued.

Although this was the last man she wanted to spend time with, especially in the sanctity of her own home, Kendra felt a softening inside her, not acquiescence, but a sort of reluctant tolerance.

"Sit down, then," she said, with zero enthusiasm.

During this exchange, Walter and Oreo were still sizing each other up, not warily, like their assigned humans, but curiously.

Ethan took a chair at the small table, looking relieved. "Thank you," he said, huffing the words out on a sigh.

Again, Kendra noted how much he'd changed physically. His temples were strangely indented, and his jaw and cheekbones protruded a little, and his usual year-around tan had faded to a whitish-gray pallor.

"Do you need a glass of water or anything?" Kendra asked, moving to open the fridge door. Keeping her distance.

Ethan shook his head. "No," he replied.

Puzzled and still unsettled, Kendra sat down across from him. *Waited.*

Maybe if she listened to whatever it was he'd come to Copper Ridge to say, he would return to Seattle. Leave her alone.

He sighed again. Heavily. And thrust his right hand through his dark hair.

"I need your help," he said, after a long and difficult silence.

Walter approached Kendra and rested his muzzle lightly on her thigh. His soft whimper very nearly split her heart straight down the middle.

Gently, she stroked the dog's golden head.

Another silence followed, charged with emotion from both sides of the table.

Then, at last, Ethan said, "I've cut ties with Desuma and Elyse."

"You told me that this morning, at the diner."

The reminder didn't seem to register with him. "That guy you were with—"

Kendra stiffened. "Never mind who I was with," she snapped. "Tell me why you're here. And don't say you want to reconcile, because there's no chance of that and you know it."

Ethan looked pained. And given his physical state, he might really be hurting.

His glance seemed to sweep from one end of the kitchen to the other before coming to rest on Kendra's face. "I'm dying," he said bluntly.

That statement struck her midsection like the business end of a well-aimed ramrod. "You're—you're *what*?"

"I have cancer," he replied. "Stage four."

Kendra felt a familiar sting behind her eyes.

This man had hurt her deeply. Broken her, in fact.

But she'd never have wished something like this on him or anyone else.

"You're telling the truth?" she ventured.

Ethan gave a rueful and completely humorless chuckle. "I'm telling the truth," he confirmed.

And Kendra believed him.

She raised her hands to her face, pressed hard at her eye sockets, trying not to dissolve into deep, shuddering sobs.

He reached across the table and squeezed her right wrist lightly before letting go.

"So you still care," Ethan remarked, almost breathing the words, rather than saying them. "At least a little."

"Shouldn't you be in the hospital or something?" Kendra asked, when, at last, she lowered her hands and looked directly into the face of the man she'd once loved without reservation.

"Until I need palliative care," he replied, "I want to keep living in the outside world."

"I'm so sorry," she said.

He smiled, but sadly. Nodded. "I have three to six months

left before I kick the bucket, according to my doctors up in Seattle," he told her, after a brief period of reflection. "I was hoping to spend part of that time making things up to you." He paused, brushed his hand through his hair again. "I shouldn't have listened to my mother and stepsister. They lied to me, for sure, but I can't honestly say I believed them. I accused you of betraying me and getting pregnant by another man because *I* was cheating, Kendra."

Was it possible to be shocked and unsurprised, at the same time?

Evidently, it was.

For the second time that day, Kendra was glad she was sitting down.

If she'd been standing, she might have face-planted in the middle of the kitchen floor. And this time, she didn't have Gage Elder to back her up.

Numbed speechless, not only because of Ethan's admission that he'd been unfaithful but also because he was *dying*, she reached down, scooped Oreo up in her arms, and buried her face in his soft, fluffy fur.

On some level, of course, she'd known Ethan was breaking their marriage vows, but at the time she'd chosen not to believe her instincts. Which was one of the reasons she no longer trusted herself when it came to romantic relationships.

"You want me to look after you?" she asked presently. "Like a nurse?"

For all her sympathy, that wasn't going to happen.

He responded with another sad effort at a smile. "No," he said. "I'll hire a caregiver or go into hospice when things get to that point. I just want a week or so to spend with you. Go on walks, with you and Walter, like we used to—watch movies together—just talk. I have so many things to apologize for. To make up for."

There would be no making up for all he'd done.

"What about Desuma and Elyse? Surely, they want to spend time with you."

Ethan shook his head. "I've cut ties with them. Permanently." He paused, chuckled, possibly because of the irony inherent in that last word.

Had he told her that before? Maybe that morning at the diner? She couldn't recall.

"Why?"

"Because they're toxic," he replied. "And before you point out that I'm toxic as well, let me say that I know that, and I'm deeply sorry. For everything. The cheating, the meanness, siding with a pair of vipers who were out to destroy my relationship with you from day one."

Kendra thought briefly of Gage. Wished she'd accepted his invitation to stay for supper, talk together, enjoy a movie on the big screen.

But that would have been putting off the inevitable, whether she'd known it at the time or not.

"Why did they hate me so much? Desuma and Elyse, I mean?"

She hadn't intended to ask that question outside the perimeters of her own brain, but it had popped out anyway.

"Jealousy," Ethan said. "And money. The bulk of my father's estate was left to me, and they didn't want you or anyone else to have access to it. They were even more concerned that we might have children, further diluting their shares of the loot." He paused again. "I don't suppose it will be any comfort to you, but they would have treated any woman I married the same way."

"Why did you permit it?" Kendra's tone was fragile. She needed to know.

Ethan gave a shrug that made his shoulders look as if they were aching. Shook his head. "Because I was an idiot," he answered. Then he arched one eyebrow and made yet another attempt at a smile. "I've been in therapy for the last six months. I was formally diagnosed as a covert narc."

"I can't say I'm surprised," Kendra admitted.

And Ethan actually laughed. A faint twinkle flickered in his eyes. "Touché," he said. "And before you ask, no. Narcissism isn't curable. The covert ones, like me, are good at hiding it. Especially from themselves."

"Wow," Kendra said, ruffling Oreo's ears, one black, one white, as he gave a small whimper and snuggled close to her chest. "I don't think I've ever met a self-confessed narcissist," she said.

"There are a few on YouTube," Ethan remarked. "Like sociopaths and even psychopaths, more than a few of them know what they are and manage to fit into normal life by monitoring their symptoms and inclinations."

Kendra shuddered slightly. Walter, still sitting beside her chair and resting his chin on her thigh, gave a little whimper. She stroked his silken back with her free hand without looking away from Ethan.

"Well," she said, "*that's* creepy."

"Agreed," Ethan replied.

"Aren't people like that abused or traumatized during childhood? Isn't that why they turn out the way they do?"

"Sometimes," Ethan acknowledged forthrightly. "But it would appear that others—including myself—are simply born that way. And I'm sure it didn't help that my dad spoiled me rotten, especially after my mom died when I was thirteen. From the day he married Desuma, Dad practically obliterated me with gifts—cars, money, fancy clothes and trips all over the world. I think he was trying to make up for marrying again."

"Yikes," Kendra muttered. Then, after a few moments of consideration, "What made you decide to change, Ethan? Was it the diagnosis?"

"We can talk about that another time," he answered.

With that, Ethan pushed back his chair and stood, wavering slightly on his feet before catching his balance.

For the first time, Kendra noticed what he was wearing.

Not one of the bespoke suits he'd mostly favored when they were together, or pricey slacks and a high-end polo shirt. That evening, he was clad in ordinary jeans, sneakers and a T-shirt with the word BEWARE printed on the front in bold letters.

Good advice, Kendra, prompted her inner voice of admittedly rare wisdom. *Beware. Ethan could be lying about everything.*

Walter instantly left Kendra to take up his post beside his master.

Kendra stood too, still holding a now-squirming Oreo in a way that reminded her of a frightened child clinging to a teddy bear.

"It's time to head back to the motel," Ethan said dully, as though he'd used up that day's quota of energy. And maybe he had. "We'll get out of your way now."

With that, he started back through the house, Walter clicking along behind him.

"I'm so sorry this is happening to you, Ethan," Kendra told him, when they had reached the front door and opened it. "I really am."

Ethan paused on the doorstep, pulled a thin lead from his pocket and snapped it onto Walter's collar. He looked as though he had more to say—maybe a *lot* more—but he refrained.

Kendra was grateful. She'd already taken in more information than she knew what to do with.

Now, she needed time to think.

She felt scattered, confused, and very, very sad.

A part of her wanted to open the door again, call out to Ethan to come back, have supper, tell her more.

Kendra overruled that part.

She had more than enough to process without adding more to the mix.

So she walked back to the kitchen, opened the door leading into her tiny, fenced yard, and set Oreo back on his tiny, padded paws.

He did some more sniffing, made his way to one of the poles supporting Kendra's clothesline, hunkered down and peed again.

So far, so good, Kendra thought.

When it came to house-training her puppy, they had a long way to go.

Still, a start was a start.

Minutes later, back inside the kitchen, Kendra washed her hands at the sink, then raided the refrigerator for the makings of a salad—romaine lettuce, cherry tomatoes, green onions, grated carrots, Feta cheese, and shredded chicken, sprinkled with tasty balsamic vinegar and a smidge of olive oil.

Once she'd eaten, rinsed her bowl and fork and popped them into the dishwasher, she headed for her bedroom, grabbed a clean nightgown from a dresser drawer and went on into the bathroom, Oreo bounding joyfully behind her.

When Kendra was stressed, she liked to soak in the bathtub, surrounded by bubbles, and read and read and read.

And that night, Kendra was definitely stressed.

Once she'd settled into the delicious warmth of her bath, and Oreo had curled up on the mat beside the tub, she reached for her current book-in-progress.

Soon, she was immersed in *Where the Creek Bends*, by a writer she'd never heard of.

For a little while, at least, she was blessedly able to forget all about the world beyond the walls of her cottage and focus on someone else's story.

Chapter 7

Stanley, Gage's alarm clock incarnate, bounded onto the bed that Saturday morning, planting both front paws square in the middle of his chest, and began happy-whining and laving Gage's face with his sandpaper tongue.

"Whoa!" Gage protested, with a laugh. "I'm awake already! Back off a little, dude!"

Stanley did so, but he was still practically dancing with the simple joy of waking up to a new day.

We humans could learn a lot from dogs, Gage thought, not for the first time.

He threw back the lightweight comforter, swung his legs over the side of the mattress, and sat up, rubbing his face with both hands.

The two foster puppies, who were probably keepers, were waiting on the hooked rug next to the bed, squirming around Gage's ankles.

That made him laugh.

He bent, scooped one up in each hand, and nuzzled their furry little faces.

"Mornin', guys," he greeted them.

In sequence, they licked his face.

He'd sprouted stubble since he'd last shaved the morning before, but that didn't seem to bother them.

After taking the puppies outside to do their business, he brought them back in and set them down, near Stanley, then headed for the bathroom.

After a quick shower, he dressed for Jack O'Ballivan's trail ride, which wasn't much different from the way he usually dressed, of course.

Jeans. A blue chambray shirt. Boots.

Run-of-the-mill cowboy gear.

There would be the party after the ride, but he figured the dress code wouldn't change much. After all, this was Copper Ridge, Arizona, not Manhattan.

Still, he mused, maybe he ought to expand his wardrobe a bit, though he couldn't imagine himself wearing a suit and tie, except maybe to a funeral or a wedding. Even the idea of khakis and polo shirts put him off.

Beneath these random, surface thoughts, Gage suddenly realized, ran a current of concern, confusion and caution.

Brewing the single cup of coffee he drank most mornings, he lowered his inner defenses to take a closer look at what he was thinking. There seemed to be some kind of sparring match going on between his conscious and subconscious minds.

It didn't take long to figure out that Kendra, along with her ex-husband, were at the center of the mental ruckus.

There were a lot of questions brewing in Gage's brain, but then it was early days, where their connection was concerned. Despite the attraction he felt toward Kendra, which had stopped him in his boot prints when he first laid eyes on her one day outside the post office, he was wary, too.

She clearly had some hang-ups, but so did he.

Gage was still wrestling with all this when he heard a car pull up outside.

Curious, hoping maybe Kendra had decided to start their day together early, he went outside.

Turned out it wasn't a car, but a truck, pulling a horse trailer behind.

Sam, one of Jack O'Ballivan's ranch hands, got out and greeted Gage with a wave and a grin.

"Brought over a horse for your gal to ride," the older man announced cheerfully. "Jack says she's the tamest one we've got, this here mare, and I do believe he's right."

Remembering Jack's promise to provide a safe horse for Kendra to ride, Gage smiled. "Thank him for me," he said, moving down the steps of the deck with Stanley hot on his heels.

Together, he and Sam unloaded the horse.

She was a pretty little pinto, not significantly larger than a Shetland pony, and, ironically, black and white, like Kendra's new puppy, suitably named Oreo.

While Gage led the mare, whose name was Polka Dot, into the barn and a waiting stall, Sam fetched the saddle from the bed of the pickup truck and followed.

"She's no ball of fire, this ole gal," Sam said, pondering the horse as she settled into her temporary quarters. "But that means she isn't likely to take the bit in her teeth and head for the tall timber, like some of them critters we've been trying to train."

Gage stifled a chuckle, amused by Sam's old-time Western vernacular. Privately, he was wondering if this animal would be able to keep up with the other horses during the trail ride.

She looked more suited to a petting zoo.

It wouldn't do if Kendra and her requested mount fell behind the others on the trail ride but, it was what it was.

Gage was looking forward to the ride.

For just a fraction of a moment, in fact, he had a hankering to return to the rodeo circuit.

He and Sam jawed for a few minutes, discussing the day ahead, which would be a lively one for sure, and then the ranch hand got back into the truck, started the engine, and made a broad three-point turn, no small trick with a horse trailer bobbing around behind him.

Once Sam had driven away, Gage checked on Polka Dot and found her comfortable, nibbling on fresh hay.

He smiled, patted the animal affectionately on the hind end, and returned to the double-wide.

The two puppies were whining in their cardboard box, so he lifted them out and let them toddle around to their heart's content, wiping up a few puddles here and there when the inevitable happened.

Then he stepped into his home office and fired up his computer, intending to juggle stocks and bonds for a while—Gage had a knack for managing money, and over the years he'd accumulated well over seven figures in investments—but he found himself googling Ethan Larkin instead.

Nothing he discovered surprised him.

Larkin was rich, well-educated, highly sophisticated.

Yada, yada, yada.

Bored, Gage logged off.

He was about to splash his face with water and brush his teeth again, in preparation for the trip to pick Kendra up in town when, once again, he heard the sound of a vehicle outside.

Curious, he diverted himself to the front door. Opened it.

To his pleasant surprise, the new arrival was Kendra.

She was wearing jeans, boots and a long-sleeved green blouse, which set off her light auburn hair nicely. Unlike his own gear, Kendra's outfit looked brand-new, and not quite broken in.

She stared at him nervously, but with a smile. "Did I get this right?" she asked, spreading her arms away from her sides. "The cowgirl thing, I mean."

"Better than right," Gage answered, with a grin.

The last time he'd seen her, she'd been pretty tense, but she looked a little more relaxed today, and that, of course, was a good thing.

A very good thing.

"Am I too early?"

Gage shook his head, still smiling. "Relax," he said. "It's all good. Want to see the horse you'll be riding today?"

She hesitated, bit her lower lip, then rustled up a smile of her own. "Sure," she replied.

At that, he and Stanley led the way toward the barn, leaving the puppies behind in the living room.

"Her name's Polka Dot," he told her, when they were inside, standing at the gate of the mare's temporary stall.

"She's adorable," Kendra murmured, reaching between the slats to pat the mare's side. "So sweet."

"I'm told she's pretty gentle."

"That's good," Kendra said.

"Why are you so nervous?" Gage asked, keeping his tone light.

Kendra kept her eyes on the mare, drew in a deep breath, and let it out in an audible rush. "My ex-husband paid me a visit last night," she replied, turning, with some effort, to look up into Gage's eyes. "It was rough."

An alarm went off inside Gage's head, but he managed to quell it. Mostly.

Whoa back, cowboy, he thought. *No need to speculate.*

"Rough?" he asked.

She nodded, and when she spoke, her voice caught in her throat. "He's dying," she said, a few moments later. "I wouldn't have believed him—he's a chronic liar—but he looks—well—*really* bad."

Gage wanted to take her into his arms and hold her tightly. Instead, he simply rested a hand lightly on her shoulder.

"I'm sorry to hear that," he said.

"Me, too," Kendra replied.

"Do you want to talk about this?"

She shook her head, rallied up a smile.

She'd been through a lot, this woman. And she was brave.

"Maybe another time, Gage. Not today, though. Today, I want to hang out with friends and have fun."

Gage wondered if what he was feeling for her right then might turn into love.

Time would tell.

"Good idea," he said. "In the meantime, I've got to put the puppies back in their cardboard cage so they don't saturate the carpet while we're out."

She leaned down to pet Stanley, who had been trying to get her attention ever since she'd arrived. When she straightened up, she was still smiling, though barely.

After they'd seen to the puppies, Gage went back to the bedroom to swap out his boots for a better pair.

When he returned to the living room, Kendra was standing in front of the picture wall, studying the portrait of Summer.

"Is this your wife?" she asked, with a gentleness that wrenched something inside Gage.

"My late wife," Gage clarified. "Her name was Summer."

"She was beautiful."

"Yeah." That gruff response was all Gage could come up with at the moment.

Kendra's shoulders stooped just slightly, before straightening again.

When she met Gage's gaze, she was smiling once more.

"We're broken people, you and I, aren't we?" she speculated, with a sad expression.

"Yeah," Gage agreed. "And that makes us normal members

of the human race, Kendra. Everybody—and I mean *everybody*—struggles at one time or another."

"You're probably right," she agreed.

He grinned, seriously considering kissing her, right there in the barn.

So romantic of him.

He was a regular romance-novel hero.

He didn't kiss her, in the end.

It was too soon for that.

Or was it?

"You ready to head for the O'Ballivans' place?" he asked, in what he hoped was the correct tone of voice.

She nodded. Her face brightened and her eyes twinkled.

"Yes. Let's saddle up, Cowboy," she said. "We've got a trail ride ahead."

Relieved, and oddly comforted by the gentleness in Kendra's tone, Gage nodded. "Yep," he agreed.

Ten minutes later, they were mounted on their horses and ready to ride.

Instead of following the road, they wound across the broad fields between Gage's place and the O'Ballivan ranch, Stanley galloping on ahead, as if to clear a path.

When they reached their destination, after twenty minutes or so, there was a lot going on.

Caterers were setting up an elaborate barbecue operation, small booths sprouting up beyond more than two dozen picnic tables with red and white plastic tablecloths flapping in the light breeze.

Within the tentlike booths, each housing a different game, teenagers were setting out prizes, some of which were pretty impressive.

Jack, who had been supervising the establishment of a spacious wooden dance floor, approached them, smiling a welcome.

"Hello, Kendra," he said. "Gage."

Harper appeared from the barbecue area, wearing a ruffled apron over her jeans and T-shirt and smiling broadly. "Kendra, you *did* it! You're back in the saddle!"

"It's been a while," Kendra replied, swinging, somewhat stiffly, down from Polka Dot's wide back. "But I think I'm getting the hang of riding a horse again."

The two women hugged.

Gage dismounted, shook Jack's hand. "Looks like this is going to be quite a get-together," he commented.

Briefly, Jack glanced back at his wife, who was leading Kendra away, toward the barbecue space. "I have a lot to celebrate," he said, so quietly that he might have been thinking aloud, instead of speaking.

It was clear that he loved Harper with everything he had.

Gage felt a stab of good-natured envy.

He wanted to love a woman like that again, and be loved in return.

He wanted kids.

Automatically, he lifted his gaze to the vast blue sky and offered a silent prayer.

Chapter 8

Fifteen minutes into the trail ride, Kendra and her mount, Polka Dot, were starting to fall behind the other horses and their riders. Gage, who had been near the front of the bunch, helping Jack set the general direction, turned his own horse in a graceful arc, rode back and fell in beside Kendra.

"Everything okay?" he asked.

Kendra felt heat pulsing in her cheeks and along the length of her neck. "Maybe I should go back," she said. "We can't seem to keep up, Polka Dot and I."

There were more than thirty horses and riders in the group, and they didn't seem to be having any issues at all, which increased Kendra's sense that she was standing out like the proverbial sore thumb.

Gage looked disappointed by that suggestion, which was both encouraging and frustrating—encouraging because he clearly wanted her to stay and frustrating because she felt like such a fool, bobbing along behind the others, bouncing in the saddle like a rubber ball on a trampoline.

"Why would you do that?" he asked, with calm concern, reining in his gelding to keep from darting ahead. "Head back, I mean?"

If this had been a movie, Kendra reflected, she'd have been the comic element, the greenhorn trying to look competent.

And, once again, she was letting her imagination run away with her.

"Like I said, I'm slowing everyone down," she said. "Plus, I feel like an idiot."

Gage smiled. "Nobody is judging you, Kendra," he pointed out, his voice kind. "I'll talk to Jack; maybe we can rustle up a faster horse."

With that, he rode toward his friend.

Meanwhile, Kendra noticed that Harper was watching, and turning her buckskin mare in her direction.

On arrival, she reined in and grinned at Kendra. "Looks like you're having some trouble. Want to switch rides?"

Kendra immediately shook her head. Harper was an experienced rider, and her horse was young and lively. "I think I'll just go back to your place," she said, very quietly, glancing briefly after Gage. "I can help with the setup or something."

Harper looked sad.

Kendra bit her lower lip.

"If you go back to the house," Harper told Kendra, "I'm going, too."

Inwardly, Kendra sighed. She couldn't drag her friend away from the trail ride. Everyone, including Kendra herself, had been looking forward to it ever since it was announced.

Gage returned, but he still looked torn. Kendra knew he was helping Jack keep the event safe for the other riders, many of whom were either new to the game or just out of practice, like she was. If something happened to spook the horses, or there was an accident of some sort, he, like Jack and several of the other men, would be needed.

"Okay," Kendra decided, albeit reluctantly, watching Harper. "I'll switch."

Harper grinned. "Great," she said, wrapping her horse's reins loosely around the horn of her saddle and slipping deftly to the ground.

Kendra dismounted and felt the familiar sting in the balls of her feet as they hit the hard dirt.

The rest of the group had stopped to watch and wait, and Kendra's face went hot all over again.

Up until today, it had been years—more than a decade, in fact—since she'd ridden a horse. She clearly wasn't ready to pick up where she left off.

So, why had she agreed to join the trail ride in the first place?

What had she been thinking?

The answers were obvious, of course.

She'd wanted to spend time with Gage Elder, even if it meant risking her neck.

Harper's mare pranced and sidestepped a couple of times as Kendra tried to stick a booted foot in the stirrup and pull herself up into the saddle by gripping the horn with both hands.

Gage finally dismounted and held the mare by one halter strap.

Mortified, Kendra finally succeeded in mounting her friend's horse.

The mare threw back her head and whinnied, as though in protest.

After that, Kendra's nerves were shot.

She rode slowly, beside Harper and Polka Dot, and no matter how she tried to relax, to go with the flow, she just couldn't.

The spirited mare was fitful, straining at the bit, clearly wanting to break loose and join the rest of the group.

Gage rode ahead, then rode back to check on Kendra, then rode back to the front again.

The cycle continued until they'd reached the landmark, Copper Ridge, after which the town had been named.

The view from there was downright spectacular.

Miles of open ranch land, with the gleaming Diamond Creek threading its silvery, sun-dappled way from one side of the valley to the other. Nearby foothills, bordered with tall trees, and snow-capped mountains in the near distance.

The scene shifted Kendra's state of mind from anxiety to absolute wonder.

She'd forgotten just how beautiful this part of the state really was. She felt her heart swell and her eyes burn.

Home.

Copper Ridge was, and always would be, her true home.

Gage, beside her now, reached over to take her hand in his.

Kendra, choked up, tried to speak and couldn't.

For reasons she couldn't have explained, her past fell away.

The early loss of her parents, and then her grandmother's passing.

Her life in Seattle.

The miscarriage.

Her failed marriage to Ethan.

Suddenly, Kendra felt ridiculously light, as if her boots were filled with high-powered helium and she might just float away into that sweeping expanse of blue, blue sky like a balloon.

Gage, still holding her hand, squeezed lightly.

"Isn't that your place?" Kendra asked, pointing to a clearing where a barn and a white structure stood.

Stanley, who, along with two or three other dogs, had joined the sojourn, let out a plaintive whimper.

"Yes," Gage answered, letting go of her hand and slipping down off his horse. He took a collapsible plastic bowl from his saddle bags, along with a canteen, and poured water for Stanley, who lapped it up in loud slurps. "Part of it, anyway."

Kendra wanted to dismount and stand beside Gage, but she

was afraid her stiff, achy legs would make it too hard to get back on the horse. She was saddle sore, for sure.

So she stayed where she was.

"Part of it?" she asked.

Gage indicated a much larger area with a sweep of one arm. "I bought the Macabee place. The closing is next week."

Kendra thought she remembered someone mentioning that Gage was buying the Macabees' ranch; Eleanor, probably.

"What are you going to do with so much space?" she asked, still feeling lighthearted. All that fresh air was lifting her spirits, despite the numbness in her feet and the throbbing ache in her thighs and backside.

"Run a few cattle," Gage answered. "And I'll probably build a house."

"Really?" In Kendra's opinion, the spacious, attractive double-wide Gage lived in now was enough of a house for anybody. It even had a fireplace, and the kitchen alone was almost the size of her whole cottage.

"Yeah," Gage replied, collecting the now empty plastic bowl, patting Stanley on the head, and returning stuff to his saddlebags. "You sound surprised."

Kendra blushed lightly. She had no business being surprised. What Gage Elder did with his property was his own business, and none of her concern.

"Want to get down? Stretch your legs?" he asked, when she didn't reply.

By then, Kendra was well aware of the fact that all the other riders had dismounted. They were laughing, chatting and sipping from water bottles while their horses grazed.

Harper, who had been alongside Kendra for most of the ride, was standing under a tree with her husband, laughing at something Jack had said.

They looked so happy, those two.

She felt a flicker of benign envy.

"No, thanks," Kendra replied, at length. "It might be hard to mount up again."

Gage chuckled at that. "You need a little practice, that's all," he assured her. "And I can help you get back in the saddle, if you want me to."

After that, they didn't talk much.

Soon, all the other riders mounted up again, ready to head back to the O'Ballivan ranch for the rest of the party.

Harper, always a good sport, didn't seem to mind plodding along, far behind all the others, and when Gage rode forward to confer with Jack, she grinned at Kendra and said, "Don't try to deny it. You've got a thing for Gage Elder."

Kendra sighed. Maybe she did. Maybe she didn't.

"He seems like a good person. We barely know each other, though."

"But there's definitely an attraction," Harper prodded, enjoying herself.

"I guess so," Kendra admitted.

Harper's smile fell away. "But your ex-husband is in town, right? Not that you told me or anything. The word is all over town."

Kendra didn't want to go into the Ethan-dilemma.

If she thought about the situation for too long, let alone talked about it, she'd be drained of energy.

And, besides, today was kind of a special day. What with the trail ride and the upcoming barbecue and all.

She didn't want to think about Ethan, let alone *talk* about him.

Kendra was just formulating a reply when the unthinkable happened.

The mare she was riding suddenly freaked out, whirling in tight circles, neighing like crazy and then bolting down the hillside at a dead run.

Terrified, Kendra couldn't do anything more than clutch the

reins in sweating hands and tighten her legs around the animal's barrel of a midsection.

She opened her mouth to scream, but no sound came out.

Picking up speed, the mare stumbled slightly, then righted herself.

The ground seemed to undulate around them as Harper's horse began to buck again, this time in earnest.

Kendra was braced to be thrown and maybe trampled in the process, but she still couldn't scream.

The reins slipped from her hands, flopping lose around the animal's legs.

And then Gage was riding beside her.

He zeroed in, grabbed Kendra around the waist with his left arm and hauled her off the mare and onto his own horse. After shifting his hold on her from his left arm to his right, he leaned in again and caught the mare by the bridle strap, holding on while she jumped and kicked.

Moments later, Jack and two other men were there, and the panicked mare was soon under control.

Kendra let the back of her head rest against Gage's strong shoulder and sucked in one deep breath after another while her heart seemed to leap around in her chest like Harper's horse. Her legs were limp, though one was wrapped around the saddle horn.

"I've got you, Kendra," Gage told her quietly, his breath warm against her cheek. "Just breathe."

Everyone was looking at her. She could feel their gazes like prodding fingers.

"Wh-what happened?" she asked. "Everything was okay and then—well—the horse went crazy."

With her head still in contact with Gage's shoulder, she felt his shrug. Instantly turned to look into his face to see if he was being impatient.

He wasn't. His expression was gentle. Calm.

"Sometimes, horses just lose it for no particular reason," he answered. "Kind of like people."

For a moment, his mouth was very close to hers.

Was he about to kiss her?

A charge surged through Kendra at the thought, but in the end, it didn't happen.

The look in his blue-green eyes seemed to indicate that he'd wanted—*still* wanted—to kiss her.

But there were too many people around, probably staring.

At least, Kendra chose to believe that was the reason he'd held back.

The ride back to the ranch and the party, which was already gearing up when they arrived, took a long time.

Jack led Harper's horse beside his own, and Harper toddled along on Polka Dot.

There were several of Jack's hired men waiting to cool down the horses and put them out to pasture for a long rest, and Kendra, still riding sidesaddle on Gage's lap, took in the scene.

Gage had kept his gelding to a brisk walk, so they were a ways behind the others.

Kendra dreaded dismounting, even though she longed to feel solid ground beneath her feet again. She was getting cramps in her legs, and she knew she'd be stiff for hours, if not days.

This saddened her, since she'd been secretly looking forward to dancing with Gage, later on, when the band struck up a lively tune and everybody headed for the improvised dance floor.

She was trying to shift her thoughts to a more positive stream when she felt Gage's lips brush lightly against her temple.

Was that—?

No, of course not.

Gage *hadn't* kissed her there.

Except that he nibbled at her earlobe next.

It was an innocuous thing, but fire shot through Kendra's entire body.

"Gage," she murmured.

When she turned to face him, it happened.

He kissed her. Full on. Hard and deep.

"Uh-oh," she said, when Gage drew back.

"Yeah," he agreed, with a sexy grin. "Uh-oh is right."

Chapter 9

"Are you all right?" Harper asked, approaching Kendra in front of the barn, a sprawling structure with multiple stalls.

Jack, Gage and a few ranch hands went off to look after the horses, while the guests who'd joined in the trail ride meandered toward the barbecue setup and the accompanying bar.

The crowd was growing larger by the minute as cars and trucks pulled in from the main road and jostled for parking spots.

Kendra sighed. "You mean, besides feeling like a complete fool?" she countered quietly. "I used to *love* riding horses. I was good at it. I even did some dressage—jumping and stuff like that. When did I turn into a bumbling misfit?"

Harper moved to Kendra's side, put an arm around her shoulders, and squeezed, briefly but firmly. "Will you *stop* beating yourself up, please?" she asked, with a touch of drama. "It's not as if you did anything wrong."

Kendra smiled at her friend, but sadly. She knew why she tended to beat up on herself; it had begun soon after she and Ethan had started seeing each other regularly.

At first, things had been good.

Ethan had been so attentive. He'd virtually swept Kendra off her feet, constantly complimenting her looks, her intelligence, her personality. He'd showered her with expensive gifts and taken her on impromptu trips to places like Belize and Hawaii and even Paris.

Nothing had been too good for his fiancée.

The moment the ring was on her finger, however, he'd changed.

Become more distant, more critical—essentially following his stepmother and stepsister's lead.

The entire scenario, according to Kendra's online therapist, had been a form of love bombing, a tactic of dedicated narcissists everywhere.

As time passed, Desuma and Elyse continued to criticize practically everything Kendra did, said, or wore. They talked a lot about Ethan's former girlfriends, and how much more suited they'd been to someone of his caliber.

His *caliber,* it turned out, had been .45, like a pistol.

By the time she'd begun—finally—to question their relationship, she was pregnant. Since she wanted a child so desperately, she'd decided to try to make things work with Ethan.

He'd been away from home more and more often, on supposed business trips, and most of Kendra's friends had begun to distance themselves from her. In retrospect, it was obvious that they'd had prior ties with the in-laws and weren't really friends at all.

Relationships with co-workers dwindled, too, because people were always getting transferred, or simply leaving the company for other enterprises.

But not Charlie Baker.

Charlie had been a software engineer, a very nice guy with a compassionate nature. Because they often shared projects at work, he and Kendra had begun to meet, very innocently, outside of work, for coffee and companionship. Sometimes, he brought his wife, Ellen, along on these get-togethers, and they all got along beautifully.

This hadn't bothered Ethan in the beginning, but when Kendra became pregnant, little by little, he became suspicious of her friendship with Charlie. Although Ellen was obviously part of the equation, Kendra's husband-at-the-time glossed over the fact that the couple had been married for more than a decade, had five kids, and still went on regular date nights together.

They were deeply in love and so committed to each other that Kendra had sometimes envied them.

Still, she'd hung on to her marriage, trying to convince herself that things would get better if she tried to be patient.

But things hadn't gotten better.

They'd gotten much, much worse.

First of all, Kendra's pregnancy had ended in a painful, heartbreaking way.

And after that, Ethan, cheered on by Desuma and Elyse, had accused her of cheating on him.

He had photos on his phone, showing Charlie and Kendra having lunch together in a café near her office. Ellen Baker had been there, with her husband, but she'd been removed from the picture.

Finally, Ethan had filed for divorce, and Kendra hadn't had the heart, hope or strength to fight for her marriage.

She'd given up, left her job, and moved back home to Copper Ridge to start over.

Hello, square one.

"Kendra?" Harper's tone was mildly anxious. "Are you still with me?"

Kendra blinked a couple of times and returned from her inner sojourn into her past. She gave a nervous chuckle and replied, "Sorry about that. I think I might have slipped into a vortex or something."

"Come with me," Harper said, tugging Kendra away from the barn, toward the crowd and then through it, in the direction of the house.

Inside, Harper gestured for Kendra to have a seat at the expansive wooden table.

"You need ibuprofen," she said, taking a plastic bottle from one of the cupboards and a bottle of cold water from the fridge. "Otherwise, you're going to be too stiff to dance."

Kendra rolled her eyes. Propped her elbow on the tabletop and placed her chin in her palm. "Dance? I think I'm going to sit this one out. Maybe go home early and soak in a tub of hot water until the muscles in my thighs stop screaming."

Harper plunked the pill bottle down on the table in front of Kendra, along with the water. "Take the recommended dose and cool your heels for a little while, cowgirl. I'm going to check on the girls and have a word with the babysitter."

She was referring to her and Jack's daughters, one an infant, one a toddler.

Their oldest, a boy named Gideon, was probably outside socializing with other kids his age, playing horseshoes or winning prizes at the game booths.

This, Kendra thought, was what a happy family looked like.

After about five minutes, Harper returned, smiling fondly. "My baby girls are fine. Janet is the *best* sitter."

Kendra didn't know who Janet was, but that didn't matter. "Ready to get back to the party?" she asked, breathing through the soft ache the very thought of having children always formed in her heart. "You're the hostess, so people are probably looking for you."

"First," Harper replied in her kindly but no-nonsense way, "tell me you took the pills. They might not wipe out the pain entirely, but they should take the edge off so you can enjoy the rest of the party."

Kendra lifted the bottle, rattled it.

"Done," she said.

Harper nodded and took the bottle, replacing it in its spot in the cupboard.

But instead of leading the way to the back door, she raised her eyebrows thoughtfully. "You know, you're not the only one around here who's been through a rocky relationship," she said, leaning back against a counter and folding her arms. "I was in love once, before I met Jack, and I caught the guy cheating with one of my friends. The pain nearly broke me, but, Kendra, I'm not telling you this to one-up you on the scale of sadness-and-suffering—I thought I'd never love another man; I wasn't willing to risk being hurt so badly again." She paused, sighed, reflecting. "Well, obviously, I met Jack, and I was attracted to him right away, though it took a while to admit it to myself. He was patient—*so* patient—and gradually, I began to trust him and the love we shared, almost from the first moment we met." She paused again, spread her arms for emphasis. "And now look at us. We have our challenges—this is the real world, after all—but we're ridiculously happy."

Kendra couldn't help smiling. She'd known some of Harper's story before, since they'd been friends for a while, but the reminder really lifted her spirits.

Not every man was like Harper's ex.

Or like Ethan.

Standing, somewhat awkwardly since the ache in her muscles seemed to be seeping into her very bones, Kendra crossed the room and gave Harper a hug.

"Thanks," she said. "I needed to hear that."

Harper beamed. "I think you've met the right guy," she confided. "I happened to look back and see the way you two kissed out there in the field."

Kendra laughed, blushed slightly. "As kisses go, that one was a winner."

"Good," Harper replied, whispering gleefully because they

were outside again, crossing the ranch house's back porch. "If the kiss was a winner, just imagine what it will be like when you and Gage make love."

A hot shiver raced through Kendra's system at the thought. She lifted one hand, palm out. "That isn't going to happen anytime soon. Gage and I are just friends at the moment."

Harper giggled. "Whatever," she said.

Once they reached the barbecue area, which was crowded with happy, laughing people, Harper and Kendra were separated, Harper greeting guests, Kendra running square into Gage, who had apparently been approaching her from behind.

"Hungry?" he asked.

Damn, even his voice was sexy.

Kendra thought of Harper's rather spicy remark and put her hands to her cheeks, trying to cool them down—and cover them.

"Starved," she said. "How about you?"

"Same," Gage replied.

Within minutes, they were in line, filling their plates with savory food.

Once they had eaten, they scoped out the various games.

Gage won a stuffed animal at one of the booths—a pink and white teddy bear—and handed it to Kendra.

She felt like a teenager at a state fair with her boyfriend.

"Thank you, Gage," she said.

He smiled, brushed a strand of her hair off her cheek and behind her ear. "My pleasure," he said.

A double entendre? Kendra couldn't know for sure, but the words sent another of those hot shivers through her.

To hide her expression, she buried her face in the teddy bear's soft fur.

"Kendra," Gage said, stopping her mid-step.

She looked up, saw that Gage was looking toward the outdoor bar.

Following his gaze, she spotted Ethan.

Ethan, of all people.

What was he doing here?

Surely, Harper would have told her if she'd invited Kendra's ex-husband to the party.

Wouldn't she?

Most likely, he had heard about the get-together in town and decided to crash it.

Not surprisingly, Ethan was looking back at them.

Slowly, weaving his way through the throng, he approached.

Kendra was stricken to silence.

Gage slipped an arm around her waist, his grip gentle but also firm.

"Quite a party," Ethan said, raising his glass in a desultory salute as he stared at Gage, a look of slow-burning fury in his eyes. "You two seem to be having a good time."

"Ethan—"

Kendra's protest died on her lips.

"We're having a great time," Gage confirmed, his tone even. Calm.

"Interesting," Ethan prodded.

"So far," Gage answered, "it's been fine." He paused, watching Ethan's response. "Is there something you wanted to say?"

Ethan wavered slightly on his feet, which made Kendra think he was probably several drinks in—or he was about to collapse from his illness.

Had he driven his rental car to the ranch, despite his obvious inebriation?

Kendra shuddered at the thought. Then she leaned into Gage's side, and he held her more tightly.

"You do realize that Kendra and I are going to reconcile?" Ethan said.

Kendra stiffened. "*What?* Ethan, that's—"

"I'm dying, you see," Ethan went on, blithely confident. "Kendra was my *wife.* And I need her help to get through it all."

Gage stiffened slightly, but he didn't look at Kendra, as she'd expected him to do. She'd imagined him demanding an explanation.

"If Kendra plans to help you, I can respect that," Gage said, very quietly. "But if she wanted to 'reconcile,' as you put it, I think she would have started the process by now."

Suddenly it seemed important—terribly important—to set Ethan straight, in Gage's presence.

"I'm really sorry for what you're going through, and I'm okay with it if you need financial help, for instance," she told her ex-husband plainly, "but there isn't going to be a reconciliation, Ethan."

Ethan looked angry; Kendra saw that he'd clenched one of his fists, and that made her pull back a little.

"So you're hung up on this—this *cowboy*, Kendra? Is that it?" He nearly spat the words.

"That's none of your business," Kendra replied, and then wondered if she'd said the wrong thing. Was she telling Gage, however indirectly, that she *was* hung up on him?

Because, she suddenly realized, she definitely was.

In fact, she was starting to believe she loved him. Or was beginning to, at least.

Though this certainly wasn't the time to say so.

"Back off," Gage warned, when Ethan took a step forward, glaring at Kendra.

Ethan stopped, gave Gage a once-over, and retreated a little.

"*I'm dying*," he said. "I *need* my wife back."

"Maybe you should have thought of that a little sooner," Gage commented. There was no hostility in his voice or his manner; he was as calm as lake water on a windless day.

Just then, Jack approached, looking apologetic. "Let's get you a ride home, buddy," he told Ethan, gripping him by the right arm and starting to steer him away. "You're in no condition to drive."

Surprisingly, Ethan didn't resist. He seemed to sag a little, so that another man stepped up and took him by the other arm.

"Find out where he's staying and take him there," Jack told the second man, who nodded and led Ethan back in the direction he'd come from.

Jack was about to say something to Gage and Kendra when Ethan stopped, turned around and yelled, "At least take care of my damn dog, if you won't help me!"

Walter. Oh, God, what was going to happen to that sweet dog?

Kendra lowered her head, fighting back tears.

That was when the band gathered, tuned their various instruments, and struck up a lively country tune.

Gage turned to face Kendra.

"Hey," he said, somewhat gruffly, extending one hand. "What do you say we have our first dance?"

Their *first* dance, as though there would be many more in the future.

Sniffling, Kendra smiled up at him. Took his hand.

"Lead the way, cowboy," she said.

Chapter 10

It was late when Gage drew his truck up in front of Kendra's cottage.

She was exhausted, not to mention saddle sore, and they'd agreed to leave her car at his place until morning, so she wouldn't have to drive.

When the truck's headlights swept across the front of the small house, Kendra gasped, and Gage muttered a swear word, hit the brakes, and thrust open his door.

Walter was sitting forlornly on the tiny porch, tied to one of the pillars by his leash. He stood when he spotted Kendra running toward him, passing Gage in her hurry, and gave a loud whimper of confusion, then a tentative bark.

"What the hell?" Gage asked, as Kendra dropped to her knees and wrapped both arms around the dog's quivering body, murmuring words of comfort.

Ethan's final words, back at the O'Ballivan place, rattled in her ears.

At least take care of my damn dog, if you're not going to help me!

He'd done it. Ethan had actually *abandoned* the pet he'd raised from a puppy.

"It's okay, Walter," Kendra told the dog, choking back a sob. "Everything's going to be okay, I promise."

Gage was gently untying Walter from the porch pillar. "Take it easy, partner," he said kindly. "We've got you."

Minutes later, inside the house, Kendra greeted an excited Oreo, who was clearly overdue for a visit to the backyard.

While Gage attended to the smaller dog, Kendra stroked Walter's maple-gold head and continued to reassure him. Tentatively, the animal leaned in and licked her face once.

Her emotions were in complete turmoil as she sat there in her kitchen, gazing at Walter. Anger, pity, heartbreak—she didn't try to identify the rest.

Yes, Ethan had deserted his dog.

But he was terminally ill, after all. And he knew that Kendra loved Walter, that she'd take good care of him.

Which, of course, she would.

After a few minutes, Gage returned, carrying Oreo in the curve of one arm. Walter was drinking water from one of Kendra's mixing bowls while she scooped kibble into another.

"Do you want me to stay the night?" he asked, clearly concerned that Ethan might show up again and cause problems. "I'd sleep on the couch, of course—"

Kendra wished she could accept the offer, but her conscience wouldn't let her.

Gage had dogs of his own to look after, and he'd need to bring his horse back from Jack and Harper's place in the morning. And, after that, he'd drive Kendra's car to town.

"That's okay," she said, with a shake of her head.

"You're sure? Your ex is obviously a loose cannon—"

"He won't be back tonight. He's probably at the motel again by now, passed out."

"Do you think he's really dying?" Gage ventured.

Kendra glanced at Walter, who was nibbling at the food she'd just given him.

Then she nodded. "Ethan is a real jerk, but he's always loved his dog. If he left him here, he's desperate."

Or, she thought, this is another manipulative tactic.

Even if he *was* trying to put one over on her, his health was clearly in decline.

He was too thin, too pale, too shaky on his feet.

God knew, Ethan had a gift for drama, though.

"How do you feel about that? His being terminal, I mean?"

"Sad," Kendra admitted. "I stopped loving Ethan a long time ago, but I do feel sorry for him. It must be awful, being so sick, and from the looks of things, he's on his own. He's estranged from what's left of his family, apparently, and if he treated his friends the way he treated me, they're probably ancient history by now."

Gage leaned down, gently placing Oreo on the floor.

The puppy waddled over to Walter's side and gave him an inspection, canine style.

"Something's happening between us, Kendra," Gage said, his tone quiet and somewhat cautious. "Am I wrong about that?"

Kendra recalled that firestorm of a kiss.

The dancing, mostly slow as the evening wore on, and how it felt to be held so close to Gage.

"No," she said. "You're not wrong."

"So where do we go from here?"

"One step forward. Then another. We need to talk, Gage, spend time together walking and"—here, she paused and, with a slight smile, winced—"going riding. If I buy a horse, can I board it at your place? And maybe you could give me a few lessons, get me back up to speed?"

He crossed the room then, stood in front of Kendra, smoothed a lock of hair back from her forehead. Then he smiled. "Yes, Kendra. To all of that. And a lot more."

Was he going to kiss her again?

He was so close.

So warm and solid.

He tilted his head to one side, grinned. "You're a very practical woman, Kendra Spencer," he said. "I like that."

She stood on tiptoe, kissed his bristly chin. Then she slipped her arms around his neck and leaned in even closer.

She was tired of holding back, watching her step, fearing the worst.

"This practical woman," she whispered, her lips so close to his that she could almost feel them against her own, "wants a practical man. Preferably, a cowboy."

Gage kissed her then, lightly this time. Then he laughed. "I'd better get out of here," he said, "before we forget we want to take things slowly."

Reluctantly, Kendra said good-night to Gage and saw him to the door.

Watched though a window as he drove away, the brake lights on his truck shining red-orange in the deep darkness of a country town at night.

Walter approached her cautiously, nudged her knee with his muzzle.

More tears came, but Kendra was smiling, too. This was and always had been Walter's signal that he needed to go outside.

After returning to the kitchen, she opened the back door, grateful for the security light above it.

Briefly, she imagined Ethan lurking out there somewhere, waiting to plead with her again, but, thankfully, he didn't appear.

Walter did his business, and once he was inside, she locked and bolted the door.

Normally, people in Copper Ridge didn't bother with that

kind of precaution, since the local crime rate was virtually zero, but, after Ethan's unexpected arrival at the party earlier, she knew she needed to secure her small cottage thoroughly.

She checked all the windows, including the one in the bathroom, high above the tub.

Walter and Oreo followed her from room to room, watching curiously as she worked the latches on every window and pulled all the curtains.

Once she was sure the whole place was pretty much impregnable, exhausted though she was, she ran a hot bath, stripped off her clothes, and slowly lowered herself into the soothing warmth of the tub.

Bubbles floated over the sides, and Oreo put on a comedy show by chasing them, leaping upon them, growling his modest little growl.

Walter, for his part, sat back, calmly watching his furry companion's antics.

Watching him watching Oreo, Kendra's heart swelled to painful proportions inside her chest, and more tears slipped down her cheeks.

Life was so complicated, she thought.

Sometimes good, sometimes bad, but mostly somewhere in between.

She said a silent prayer, soaked a while longer, and then climbed out of the water, dried herself off with a thirsty towel, and put on an oversized T-shirt, her nightgown of choice.

In the kitchen, she placed Oreo in his cardboard box for the night.

He nestled in without complaint, and Kendra kissed her fingertips and placed them on top of his head.

Then, after brushing her teeth and smoothing moisturizer on her face, she headed for her bedroom.

The covers were lightweight, since it was summer in Arizona, and, after switching off the lamp beside the bed, Kendra nestled beneath them, centering herself in the middle of the mattress.

It took a few moments for her to realize this was unusual; even after her divorce, she'd slept on one side of the bed for months, carefully saving space for a man who wasn't there.

Tonight, she wanted that space for herself.

And then Walter. Because he joined her after a few inquiring whimpers and a leap that made the whole bed shake when he came in for a landing.

Kendra laughed.

Hugged him.

He lay down next to her, atop the covers, his sturdy body warm against her own.

Gently, she stroked the dog's fur until his even breathing indicated that he'd fallen asleep.

When she awakened early the next morning, still a little sore from yesterday's trail ride and her debut as bucking-bronc rider, Kendra felt a number of emotions sweep over her in quick succession.

Sadness and sympathy for Ethan, of course, but there was also hope. For herself, for Gage.

Maybe, just maybe, she was getting a second chance at love and life with Gage.

Scrambling out of bed, because Oreo was yipping in the kitchen and Walter had just bounded to the floor to stand staring at Kendra and bumping at the side of her knee with his muzzle, she purposely set aside her usual habit of wondering what would go wrong in the next twenty-four hours, and hummed as she attended to her duties as a dog owner.

After they'd been outside, and she'd refilled their food and water bowls—careful to put Oreo back into his box to eat—Kendra showered, dressed and consulted the calendar feature on her smartphone.

She wasn't working that day, and she had no appointments,

though she planned to go over her various investments online, since that was her main source of income.

Her waitressing job was purely therapeutic, a reason to get out of the house and interact with other people.

She had just finished a quick assessment and logged off when she heard a knock at the front door.

At first, Kendra was alarmed.

Was Ethan back—maybe to reclaim Walter and take him away?

The thought made her dread answering the knock.

After a cautious peek out of a side window, though, she was pleased to see Gage waiting on the doorstep.

He'd returned with her car, as promised, and spotting her peering at him, he grinned, raised the key ring, and made it jangle.

Kendra opened the door, Walter at her side.

Was he waiting for Ethan to come fetch him?

The thought broke her heart.

But when Gage bent to ruffle Walter's ears, the dog, tail wagging and tongue lolling, seemed happy to see him.

Straightening up again, Gage smiled at Kendra and handed her the key chain.

"Thanks," she said, pocketing it.

Gage leaned in and kissed her lightly, tantalizingly, on the lips.

"How about a ride home?" he asked.

"How about some breakfast first?" Kendra countered.

Gage arched one eyebrow, and his blue-green eyes danced. "Are we talking about yogurt and muesli?" he wanted to know. "Because, pardon me, but that ain't cowboy food."

"Bacon and eggs," Kendra informed him. "Plus hash browns."

"Now, you're talking," Gage teased.

"But don't get too used to it," she replied. "A healthy diet is important."

Looking solemn, Gage saluted. "Yes, ma'am," he said.

And then they both laughed.

After sharing a meal and cleaning up afterward, then loading both Oreo and Walter into the back seat of Kendra's car, they headed for the wide-open spaces, their hearts singing a silent duet.

Epilogue

One year later

Spencer House looked almost new, and somehow pleased with itself, standing tall in the bright June sunshine.

Six months before, Kendra and Gage had been married there, in front of the ornate gazebo in the backyard.

Since then, several other couples had followed suit, and more than a dozen weddings were booked for the coming months.

Turning the long-empty mansion into a popular wedding venue/B&B had taken a lot of time and money, and Kendra had long since given up her job at the Hot N Tot Diner to meet the demands of a thriving business.

Now, her days were even busier than before, but she was happier than she'd ever thought possible.

"This grand old house has come to life again," Eleanor remarked. Standing beside Kendra, the older woman smiled. "Your grandmother would be so proud."

Kendra's heart swelled and she nodded in agreement. "She would."

Eleanor, now Kendra's business partner, reached out and gave Kendra's hand a light squeeze. "She'd be happy for you and Gage, too."

Kendra nodded again and started toward her car, parked nearby on the street. "I agree."

She wanted to get home.

Her husband was waiting.

"How's the new place coming along?" Eleanor asked.

Kendra laughed. As if restoring Spencer House to its former glory hadn't been challenge enough, she and Gage were having a new house built on the ranch, along with a barn.

"It should be finished soon," she replied. "We're moving in next week."

She opened the car door, slid into the driver's seat. "You don't mind sticking around to get the weekend guests settled in?" she asked.

Eleanor was certainly competent, but she was still pursuing her real estate career part-time, and she was getting older, after all.

"Don't give it another thought," she said confidently.

Kendra thanked her friend, started the car, and headed for home.

When she pulled in between the ramshackle barn and the fancy double-wide, which would soon be occupied by Tyler Fallon, the recently hired ranch foreman, and his wife, Tina, Gage was leading two horses out of the barn.

He grinned and nodded in greeting.

The dogs, Walter, Stanley and Oreo, barked wildly from inside the double-wide. Reluctantly, Gage had allowed his sister, Sophie, to adopt the other two pups, and they were now living happily in Phoenix.

Kendra approached her husband, rose onto the balls of her feet, and kissed his stubbly chin. "Hi, handsome," she said.

He laughed. "Hello, beautiful," he replied. "Ready for a ride?"

Kendra widened her eyes at him, and he laughed again.

"On *horseback*," he clarified.

"Well, that, too." Kendra chuckled.

Then she turned to admire her beautiful pinto mare, Primrose. Patting the horse's neck, she recalled the day of the trail-ride, over on the O'Ballivans' ranch, when she'd nearly been thrown. She'd come a long way since then, not only as a rider, but as a woman and now a wife.

This time, for real.

She thought briefly of Ethan, and how he'd confronted her that night at the party, and later left Walter on her front step.

Ethan had died six weeks later, in Seattle, and while Kendra no longer loved him, she hoped he would rest in peace.

Gage stood behind her and, as if sensing her thoughts, he leaned in and kissed the side of her neck lightly.

"I love you," he told her.

She turned, slipped her arms around his neck and replied, "And I love you, Gage Elder. So very much."

For a long moment, they stood in silence, just looking at each other.

Just *loving* each other.

Then, after Gage had let Walter and Stanley out of the double-wide, he watched with a sort of amused appreciation as Kendra mounted Primrose, gathering the reins loosely in her left hand.

Gage approached his gelding, Max, and mounted up.

"It's a bummer leaving Oreo behind," he said, with kindly regret.

"He'll be all right," Kendra said, reaching over to pat her husband's muscular forearm.

They rode together past the barn and the fenced corral into the wide, grassy expanse of land between there and the ridge overlooking the entire valley.

"Race you to the creek and back," Kendra said, prodding Primrose's sides lightly with the heels of her boots.

"You're on," Gage replied, and when both horses burst into a hard run, he threw back his head and laughed.

Kendra, now as at ease in the saddle as she was on her yoga mat, due to months of practice, leaned forward and nudged Primrose again.

Gage seemed to sail along beside her, rimmed in sunlight, neither pulling ahead nor falling back, though Kendra knew he would have won if they'd actually been competing.

The creek glimmered in the distance, like a wide silver ribbon binding a great gift—the gift of true, lasting love.

Their love.

One More Summer with You

MAISEY YATES

Chapter 1

When everything falls apart, there's always Camp Low Echo.

That had been the dry rallying cry of her teenage years. Jane Cahill had been sent to camp the first time as an angry, bitter girl. Spiteful. A few other things too. She'd been angry and bitter and spiteful all the time, but being all of that out in the middle of nowhere had been a novelty at least.

At first she'd been certain she'd die.

In some ways, she had.

The Jane Cahill who'd been on a path of self-destruction, that Jane had died somewhere during that first summer.

At first she'd wanted to go back to her normal life. To the school where she had all her friends, to parties and losing herself in the oblivion of alcohol. But she'd run away from every foster home she'd ever been in, and that meant the authorities had to find something to do with her. The summer she was fifteen, she'd been sent to Low Echo, a camp for troubled youths. Which had had the potential to be one of two things. Hideous, or a great time. Just depending.

It hadn't been either; at least, not in the way that she'd imagined.

Because when she thought of a great time, she thought of the mayhem she and other teenagers like her could create when left to their own devices. When she thought of hideousness, she thought of either boredom, or the possibility that the camp was one of those awful, abusive places where troubled teens were parked for the summer.

But the ranch was run by Linda and Alden Rush, who actually wanted to help. It had taken Jane the whole first summer to accept that the Rushes were good people. That they cared. There just hadn't been anyone in her life who did before.

She also met Spencer that first summer, but she was doing her best not to think about him as she waited in a chair in the front office, expecting to get her cabin assignment from Alden himself.

Linda had died four years ago.

She took a sharp breath, doing her best not to think about that funeral or that rainy June day. The way tears had fallen down her cheeks to join the rain.

How she turned around and saw him standing at the back. White cowboy hat on his head. Looking more beautiful at thirty than he had at eighteen.

Grief and regret and everything else all mingling together.

She forced her mind back to the present. She had enough going on without getting lost in the past.

Of course, that was kind of tricky when she was surrounded by so many reminders of her past.

During the funeral, she hadn't had a chance to really speak with Alden. There had been at least five hundred people in attendance. So many people whose lives have been touched by Linda. Jane was just one of many.

It had been important to her to pay her respects.

Important that she'd given Alden a hug.

But there hadn't been time for a conversation. The funeral hadn't been at Camp Low Echo. She frowned. She wondered if seeing her would be difficult for Alden, because the last time they had seen each other had been at the funeral. But when they'd spoken on the phone, he sounded like his old self.

Even if his voice was just a little bit thinner. Evidence, maybe, that Linda had taken part of him with her when she left.

Jane looked down at her hands. She could remember doing that all those years ago—sitting in one of these plastic chairs, staring at her chipped nail polish. Now she had a smooth, natural manicure that she wasn't going to be able to keep up over the summer. She wasn't sure why she'd bothered to get her nails done before she'd left.

Jane looked at the cowboy lamp sitting on the side table to her right. A man clinging for dear life to the back of a bucking horse, cast in bronze. It was the same lamp that had been here the very first time she'd found herself in this office.

So much was the same.

Even the gnawing desperation in her stomach that she'd hoped never to feel again.

She was a lawyer now. Engaged.

She looked at her left hand, at the pear-shaped diamond there, and waited to feel something, but her whole mind and body had been blank since Colin had told her they needed to postpone the wedding so that he could reevaluate his life and himself, what he wanted.

Cold feet.

That was what her boss had said. And she'd cared what he had to say because he was a mentor—or at least she'd thought he was, before she found out she'd been blocked for a promotion because she was just so valuable working on his team that he didn't want her moving up in the ranks.

She'd been cut off at the ankles by Colin, then at the knees by her boss. Everything felt vile and uncertain. Everything she'd worked for was at risk. Everything she'd hoped for, planned for, dreamed for—

"Jane."

She looked up, and there he was. Older, lines deep and pronounced on his face. Not as sad or gray as he'd been at the funeral. Alden Rush. The one man in her life she'd always considered a father figure. The only person on earth who loved her just as she was.

She stood up and reached for him, hugging him as if no time had passed.

"Oh, it's so good to be here," she said.

"It's great to have you," Alden said, stepping back and holding her by the shoulders, smiling so that his white mustache curved. "The kids are going to be so excited. Fresh blood."

She laughed. "I'm familiar with that brand of excitement."

"I know you are. It's why having you here is so important. You know who these kids are, Jane. You know how they are. You know what they're feeling."

"I don't know about that," she said, but right at this moment she felt a lot closer to the girl she'd been than she had for a long time.

"I'm looking forward to getting my cabin assignment."

It wasn't lost on her that this time at Camp Low Echo was a lifeline, just as it had been back then. As a fifteen-year-old, she had been at the end of her rope—even if she hadn't known it, and now her life was pulling itself apart, falling into pieces again.

But she still had Camp Low Echo.

The single best thing that had ever happened to her.

And if there was a large pit in her stomach related to the one thing about camp that had never been resolved, well, there was nothing she could do about that.

"We didn't get to talk really last time I saw you," Alden said, leading her out of the office, and out the front door. It was already warm. In early June. It was shaping up to be a dry, hot summer in southern Oregon. It was always a little cooler out here, in the woods near Crater Lake, but the days still got hot enough. The air smelled like wood and pine, and dragonflies buzzed in loops around her. She stopped and smiled. Dragonflies made her think of Linda. But she wasn't going to mention that.

"No," she said. "We didn't."

"I heard you're a fancy lawyer now."

All of her insecurities intruded then, threatened to close in on her. She wasn't what she'd dreamed of being at this point in her life. She also wasn't what everyone who knew her at fifteen had thought she'd be—dead in a ditch.

Even here and now, her memories of the girl she'd been felt disconnected.

As if she was looking at two different people. She could see teenage Jane clearly, but the path from that girl to where she was now made no sense. Not even to her.

She didn't give herself credit for that journey. She didn't think: *Oh, look how far I've come.*

Not ever.

"I don't know about fancy."

She had ended up at a big law firm, where she rarely had the chance to represent clients at trial. Mainly what she did was prepare casework for the partners. She was ready for something more. Had been for a while. She had earned the right to take on more responsibility. But it just wasn't happening. Not now.

Nothing was happening. She pushed that thought to the side.

"You're going to be in Squirrel Six," he said.

Each grouping of cabins was named after a woodland animal, and then numbered. Squirrel Six was the cabin where she'd lived as a teenager.

"Did you do that on purpose?"

Alden shook his head. "No. What do you mean?"

"That was a cabin I always had."

"Oh. I wish I had done it on purpose. But I never had anything to do with the cabin assignments."

She looked around at the buzzing dragonflies. No. Of course not. That was Linda.

She was caught between feeling cynical and believing in magic. The years since camp had brought their share of both. And of course the years before had just been rough.

But at camp she had always been able to put her pain away.

She'd been a kid here, for the very first time. And a woman.

Okay. She needed to stop thinking about that.

"Well, it's a happy coincidence." She wasn't sure she believed in coincidences. Part of her wanted to. Especially after the past months, when it seemed that no matter how hard you worked to achieve your goals, life was just a series of car crashes you had to endure.

She'd believed that life is what you make of it. That was what had gotten her through. It was what had gotten her through a neglectful childhood, during which she'd been passed from one family to another. It was what had given her reason to hope. But now she was struggling.

The dragonfly and the cabin assignment made her smile, though.

Alden walked with her down the familiar path, shaded by pines that reached up toward a clear blue sky.

"Your girls will be here soon. Six of them. First years."

"First years," she said. "Well." She wondered about those girls. What was going on in their lives to have brought them here. Whether there was anything she could do to help. If there was one thing she could tell them, it was . . . Okay. Maybe she wasn't quite the success she wanted to be. But the reality was that she had broken the cycle of failure in a lot of ways.

Maybe she should remember how far she'd come instead of keeping teenage Jane so separate from her current life.

There. She had gained some perspective already. A lot more than she had when she was sitting in her apartment in Chicago.

Maybe she could be of some use to somebody. Maybe she could be an example.

Perspective was everything, after all.

Hers had been severely damaged of late.

There was nothing wrong with having big dreams. No. That was another thing she had learned here at camp.

Kids from her sort of circumstances were allowed to dream. Just like everybody else. That was what she would teach the girls this summer. Yeah. She was going to teach them that.

"I was surprised you could take time out of your busy schedule to spend the summer here."

"Yeah. I . . . I took a bunch of my vacation time that I hadn't taken before." She wasn't being totally honest.

She had had a month of vacation time stored up, and she had taken it. There were three months of camp. She hadn't definitively committed to all three months, but she figured at the end of the month she would either quit the law firm, or she would have to make arrangements to go back.

And maybe Colin would call. Or maybe he would still be trying to decide what he wanted to do with his life.

They weren't *not* engaged. But they no longer had a wedding date. They had lost a bunch of deposits. She couldn't afford to quit her job right now. She also wasn't sure she could afford to stay.

She had no idea whether her life in Chicago was going to be there a month from now.

For the first time, she didn't really have a plan.

Ever since her third summer at camp—really since the second summer—Jane had always had a plan.

This drifting, uncertain feeling reminded her of being fifteen.

She did not like that.

She heard footsteps coming from a side trail and looked up, expecting to see another staff member. But when she saw who it was, her stomach tightened. Dropped all the way to her toes.

This wasn't just another member of camp staff.

It was the very ghost of camp past.

Spencer Quinn.

In all his glory.

Chapter 2

If the woman in front of him wasn't so different from the ghost of Jane that he conjured up on nights when he couldn't sleep, Spencer might have thought he was hallucinating.

He'd caught one glimpse of her at the funeral four years ago. Wearing fancy clothes, looking like the girl he'd once known dressed up in a Halloween costume, quite frankly.

He'd spent the years since then imagining lawyer Jane.

That version of her. With expensive fabrics, demure gold earrings, her hair pulled back into a bun. This wasn't that version of her.

She was wearing a blue shirt with the Camp Low Echo logo, a pair of khaki shorts that showed off her long, tanned legs, and very little makeup. Her dark hair was pulled back in a high ponytail, and she had a ring on her left hand. He noticed the ring almost right away. It did something to him. Grabbed him and chomped down hard. It was visceral. Damaging. It also made him think . . .

Did he actually care? A ring. What did he care if there was some other man in her life?

He'd dreamed of having her again, having her in his arms, at least one more time.

Did it matter that there was another man? This was camp, this was summer. That guy never had to know, and Spencer certainly didn't need Jane to make any kind of emotional commitment.

He just wanted that night all those years ago to be something more than the last time.

You really couldn't be any more pathetic.

He'd vowed never to be that pathetic over a woman again. To his credit, he hadn't been in a real relationship with anyone else.

It was always only her.

He'd felt this same upheaval when he'd seen her at Linda's funeral. That he'd been so disturbed in the midst of all that sorrow had made him angry then, and it didn't do much to help his mood now.

Jane Cahill. His one and only attempt at love.

Meeting her had been like getting shot full in the chest with a shotgun blast. Truth be told, there were still remnants of his love for her inside him. Pieces of buckshot that would never fully be removed.

Didn't mean he had to like it, romanticize it, or make it anything but what it was.

He didn't want those feelings inside him anymore.

He hadn't chosen them.

Hadn't chosen this desire that had grabbed hold of his throat at fifteen and loomed over him ever since.

There had been any number of women since Jane. There was no reason why she should be his lodestar for desire. For sex. For need.

"Spencer," she said.

He wanted to say something cool and acerbic. Say he was

surprised she could identify him after ghosting him when they were eighteen.

He didn't, though. He wasn't sure if that was maturity, the better part of valor, or if she'd actually succeeded in leaving him tongue-tied. Like the inexperienced adolescent he'd been when they'd met.

Oh, he hadn't been inexperienced physically. A hard life had led to his making hard decisions at an early age.

But emotionally? He'd had no experience with that stuff. Not with attachment or love or anything remotely resembling either one.

"Jane," he said.

He figured it was best to return fire with like fire.

"Oh hell, it's a reunion," Alden said. "I didn't realize that you knew each other."

"We do," Spencer said. "We spent the same three summers here."

"Yes," Jane said. "We did."

"Well, that's great. There are a few other people from your class working here too."

Their class. Alden loved to talk about camp that way. But in many ways, it was true. This had been his real school. There was a reason that he made arrangements to devote a month to the camp every summer. Even though he didn't actually have time to do it. All the same, he sank a lot of money into having someone cover for him at the ranch so that he could give back.

He owned land now.

He wasn't in prison.

What Alden and Linda had given him was something he could never put a price on.

Which meant he would give back in any way he could.

But he hadn't counted on Jane.

Well, why would Alden tell him? Alden had hosted thousands and thousands of kids over the years. He probably had to sit and think really hard about which kids had been in which summer groups.

There were often little cohorts, kids who got to know each other over the course of years, but there were some kids who only came once, some who came every year they could.

Alden certainly wouldn't know about Jane's significance to Spencer. There was absolutely no romance allowed at camp.

Which meant there was a hell of a lot of romance that happened at camp.

No dates, which meant they found ways to make them.

No kissing. Which meant there were some well-established make-out spots.

Absolutely no sex.

But they'd sure found their ways.

He couldn't admit that to Alden, though.

He did use his experience to make the boys' lives difficult, though. Because he knew all the sweet spots in camp.

Of course, they'd probably just found new ones.

Teenagers were going to find a way to fool around with each other, no matter what.

He'd read somewhere that with the advent of smartphones, youths were getting up to nonsense less and less these days.

Well, a lot of the kids that came to this camp weren't in a demographic that could afford smartphones, which meant they were outliers to that statistic. The trouble with sex was it was free.

Of *charge*, anyway. Not of consequences.

He looked at Jane, and his stomach tightened.

No. It was not free of consequences.

"What brings you out this summer?" he asked.

He should just let them pass. Should just let Alden carry on with showing her whatever he was showing her. But he didn't want to. He was caught between two desires.

One to keep his distance, and one to never let her out of his sight again.

Things with Jane had always been tricky like that.

Jane looked at him, her eyes still round and shocked. As if he was the one who was out of place rather than she. "I'm—"

"Walk along with us," Alden said. "We're headed to Squirrel Six."

Spencer didn't argue with Alden. He was about the only person on the planet Spencer didn't argue with.

So he went along with him.

"I had a lot of vacation time stored up," she said. "And I've been wanting to get back here."

She was lying. He could tell. He'd always known when Jane was lying. He knew so much about her. The way she smiled, the way she laughed. The way it felt to touch her. Kiss her.

He could remember, clearly, the first time he'd ever seen her.

Wearing low-cut skinny jeans and a top that fell off one shoulder. She had the worst attitude of anyone he'd ever encountered.

And he had been ready to match it tit for tat.

It wasn't as if he'd been *happy* to be sent off to camp.

His parents had acted baffled by his behavior. They just didn't know what to do with him.

They didn't admit to the fact that his dad was a drunk who took his anger out on his kids. Used his oldest son as a whipping boy. No. Because his dad had been so respectable.

They'd sent him to camp to save face because he was causing trouble all around town, and they'd wanted to look as if they were doing something about it.

Truth be told, going to camp hadn't straightened him out the way they wanted. They thought it would be a military type thing. Something to make him compliant. Instead, it had made him think.

About his future, about the way his choices were affecting it.

About what he wanted.

Camp was the greatest gift—maybe the only gift besides creating him—that his parents had ever given him.

It had directed him far away from what they'd wanted for him. From what they'd been.

He found that manual labor was the answer to a lot of his problems.

That being outdoors made him feel less like he needed to break things.

Which meant that being a banker like his dad was out of the question. Not that his dad had been some fancy city banker. He had been the manager of a small-town branch. But in their community, that had made him someone important, so he'd acted as if he was God's gift to absolutely everyone.

His dad didn't make things, though. Spencer did.

He ranched. He cultivated the land. Animals. Food. He built things. Mended fences, raised barns.

It was real.

That had changed him. Learning what kind of man he wanted to be. Camp Low Echo had helped him figure out what kind of man he wanted to be.

But he'd be lying if he didn't admit that Jane Cahill was the first person who'd really prompted him to consider what kind of man he wanted to be.

And then she'd gone and gotten too fancy for him. Her ambitions were too big.

Which was why she'd had to leave.

Couldn't stay in Oregon with the likes of him.

Not when she had places to go and important things to do.

It wasn't really fair of him to be bitter about that. Well. He didn't much care about being fair, he had to admit. Part of him was proud of her. Part of him was angry.

All of it was confusing.

The truth was, it was better that she'd gone and gotten an education. The truth was, with a whole lot of hindsight and maturity, he could see she'd been right to leave. He reserved the right to be hurt about how she'd left, though.

Without a word. After giving him the best night of his life.

He couldn't think about that right now.

"Spencer comes every year," Alden said.

"Yeah," he confirmed. "I do."

Jane looked at him, and it was like a punch to the gut. All those memories were so close now. So, so close.

"I didn't know that."

"Yeah. I pretty much have, ever since I stopped coming as a camper."

"Oh."

"I just live an hour away. I have a ranch."

Was that bragging? Well, then he was bragging. It was easy for Jane to say she was a lawyer, and that proved she had done something with herself in the time since they'd last met.

It was a lot harder to say "I'm a cowboy," and expect that it communicated the same level of success. For many people, a man wasn't a man if he didn't own land.

So saying that he owned a ranch let her know that he hadn't sat around and done nothing in the years since they'd last seen each other.

"That's . . . that's great. I work at a law firm in Chicago."

He knew. That was the problem. He'd looked her up before the funeral and after.

He was a little bit too up in her business.

God help him.

Sometimes he poured himself a glass of whiskey and asked: *What's Jane up to?*

He'd missed the ring though.

Maybe because he hadn't gone on an online spelunking expedition in a while.

He'd been trying to give it up.

Or maybe it was behind posts that were only for friends.

They were not friends. Not on anything.

He was more social media lurker than social media *haver*. And he would never, ever admit that he'd looked.

"Since y'all know each other," Alden said, stopping in the path, "I think it would be a good idea to have your teams join up for the games."

Oh, hell. The games. Boys' cabins and girls' cabins were always teamed up for them. They were fun, and normally Spencer didn't care who he was paired with. But right now? He couldn't decide if this was the best outcome, or the worst.

He'd spent fifteen years trying to get over her, and now she'd come crashing back into his life, and they were going to be on the same team.

He might feel strongly about it, but he wasn't going to let her see it. He'd let her see his feelings once. It was one time too many.

"Well, I guess that makes us teammates, Jane."

Her eyes met his, and her cheeks turned pink. "I guess it does."

Chapter 3

Right after Alden made his proclamation about teaming up for the games, he and Spencer went off to see to some mysterious tasks while she was left to settle in.

She remembered Squirrel Six better than she remembered any of the childhood dwellings that she could've called home.

She looked around the room, where all of the windows were open to let a cross breeze waft through. There was no air-conditioning in these cabins. There were three bunk beds, and a counselor bed. Three dressers with six drawers, three drawers for each girl. And one smaller dresser and a nightstand for the counselor. There was no bathroom. Everyone had to use the communal bathrooms and showers. The one for the boys was at one end of the camp, the one for the girls at the other.

She had a map of this place in her head.

It was weird to be an adult here though.

Especially weird because it was so easy for her to call back the feelings she'd had back then. Of being tender and lost and alone, covering it up with anger and defensiveness. And attitude that was embarrassing when she looked back on it, because it was just so transparent. Any adult with even cursory psychological training would have recognized it for what it was.

Fear. Weakness.

She'd been filled with those feelings back then.

She liked to think she wasn't now.

Maybe that was delusional. She didn't think she was delusional.

As she began to put things away, folding her camp clothes and putting them in drawers, she let herself go over the steps that had led her here.

Everything in her life was crumbling. Maybe she was wrong to think the answer was here.

But it was the only place she knew to go looking for it.

Spencer.

Had she been an idiot not to realize that Spencer would be here? No. She wasn't at camp every summer, she hadn't been back here since she was eighteen. Why would she have assumed that Spencer would be here?

She hadn't even thought about him.

Liar.

She did think about Spencer. Sometimes. She thought about Spencer and moments that shamed her. When life with Colin felt staid and steady, and she felt she had lost all the wildness she'd once had. That had been her goal after all.

But sometimes she didn't feel like herself. Maybe that was why she couldn't see the steps between herself and teenage Jane. The path that should connect the Jane she was now with the one she'd been back then just wasn't there, and maybe it had to do with that conscious decision to become a tamer, more palatable version of herself.

Spencer Quinn represented something wild. Something she'd had to walk away from. Staying with Spencer Quinn would have led to nothing but teenage pregnancy and a repetition of cycles that neither of them wanted to repeat.

Just thinking about that now, though, made her ache.

She was in a better place—she knew that. But there was something beige about her life. It was a little bit too comfortable compared to the heat, the vibrant colors, the wildness of her time with Spencer.

She really didn't need to go romanticizing it. She needed to get her head on straight. And it was a good thing she did, because just as she put the last of her things away, she heard her campers outside.

An older woman whom Jane had never met before arrived with the group of six girls. She had a clipboard and a no-nonsense look on her face. The girls standing behind her looked subdued if not entirely cowed by her presence.

"Evie, Peyton, Aaliyah, Keira, Olivia and Bella. Welcome to Squirrel Six." With each name, she made a checkmark on her clipboard, and Jane paid close attention to the way each girl reacted as the name was said, so she was reasonably certain she knew who was who without introductions. The woman didn't introduce herself, and she didn't linger.

She left the girls with Jane, who stood there reminding herself that she was not one of them, but was in fact the person in charge of them. She didn't have very much experience with kids of any age. Much less surly teenagers.

And based on their expressions, they were an interesting mix of surly, terrified and downright combative.

Peyton and Bella looked ready to conspire. Evie, Aaliyah and Olivia were grouped together, and she could see that they would be joining forces to make her life difficult. Keira stood alone, her dark eyes wide and uncertain.

"Well," Jane said. "Come into the cabin." She turned away and walked through the front door, holding it open, not letting it swing shut until the last girl came in. "This is Squirrel Six. It's going to be your home for the rest of the summer. And it was . . . my home for three summers."

Aaliyah raised an eyebrow. "It was?"

"Yes," she said. "I attended this camp when I was a kid. When I was your age. None of you have ever been here before, right?"

"No," Bella said out loud, while the rest of them just shook their heads.

"I remember my first summer. I was worried. And mad. Because I wanted to be somewhere else. Anywhere else. I definitely didn't want to be in the middle of nowhere. I didn't even own a cell phone, but I was still mad that I was out here without Internet."

"They take your phones," Olivia muttered.

"I know," Jane said. "I might not have had a phone for them to take, but I'm familiar with the rules." And then she said something that might be a miscalculation, something she might regret, but she was desperate for common ground, for something else to say, so she decided to give it a try. "This is my first year as a counselor. I'm familiar with camp, but not with this side of it."

So, now they would either see her as fresh blood, or maybe they would respect her because she was closer to being one of them. The decision was made. She couldn't go back and make a different one.

"What is there to do around here?" Bella asked, kicking the edge of one of the bunk beds.

"The first thing to do is choose your bed. It's going to be an important part of your summer, after all."

There was a mild scuffle, as the battle for top or bottom bunk ensued, and Jane had flashbacks to her first year, when, like Keira, she had ended up with a bed she didn't want. Keira didn't have to say anything, Jane could tell.

"What were you in for?" Aaliyah asked from her position on the top bunk.

"It's not prison," Jane replied.

"Well, I know," Aaliyah said, rolling onto her back, tilting her head back over the edge of the bunk bed as she examined Jane upside down. "Still. Something got you sent here."

"I ran away from all of my foster homes," Jane said. She looked around the room. "Anyone else?"

Aaliyah, Bella and Evie raised their hands. "So, you get it. There's a point where they don't have anywhere else to send you, and they don't know what to do with you."

"And they don't want to try to figure out why you might be running away," Bella said.

"No," Jane agreed. "Because the system is broken. People who get involved in it don't actually want to help. Alden is an exception, though."

"He's the old man we all met when we got here?" Peyton asked, her tone filled with skepticism.

"Yes," Jane said. "And I know. When I first met him and his wife, Linda, I thought they were just like everybody else. Doing it to make themselves feel good, which is honestly the best motivation you find out there. The rest are people who are desperate to try to indoctrinate troubled youths, or looking for a way to turn teens into unpaid labor, or worse still, just abusers looking for bodies that no one cares about. But they weren't. Linda died a few years ago, but Alden is still here. He's still a good man. I promise you, this camp can help you if you let it."

"Oh yeah?" Aaliyah asked. "How?"

"It let me be happy for a while. And when I was happy for long enough, not afraid of where I was going to sleep, or what was going to happen to me if I did fall asleep, I was able to dream. Think about what kind of person I wanted to be. Then I was able to start planning for it. There are a lot of people here who will talk to you about your future. About what you want, about what you can be. They did it for me—they'll do it for you."

"So, what did you end up doing?"

"I'm a lawyer," Jane said.

"Like family law?" Olivia asked, looking at her as if she was the potential scum of the earth.

"No. Not family law. I know that good attorneys are important in family law, but for a lot of reasons, I don't particularly want to get involved in that part of the system."

"I've never met anybody good in family court," Olivia said.

"I'm sorry," Jane said.

"Isn't it really expensive to go to law school?"

Jane shrugged. "Yes. I got scholarships. Being at this camp helped with that. I was able to get a letter from Alden, and he talked about how much progress I'd made. About how hard I was working, and how far I'd come."

Bella pointed at Jane's left hand. "Are you married?"

"No. Engaged."

She was pretty sure.

"That's a huge ring."

"Yeah. It is."

"In my neighborhood, somebody would steal that," Evie said.

"Well, if the ring goes missing in the middle of the night and you disappear . . . I'll wish you luck."

"So, no wonder they want you back. I mean, now you're rich and fancy, so you're here to convince all of us that if we stick to the program, maybe we will be too," Aaliyah said, her tone combative.

"No. Believe it or not, Alden didn't ask me to come back. I asked him. Because I care about this place. Because I believe in it."

"You're not really one of us," Aaliyah said. "You're just a do-gooder."

She gritted her teeth together. "Okay. You want the truth?"

All six girls stared her. "My marriage is postponed. My fiancé got cold feet. And I didn't get a promotion that I really wanted."

"Oh," Aaliyah said. "So he's a man-child."

Jane laughed. "Yes. He is kind of a man-child. And I needed to get away for a little while. So maybe I'm not a do-gooder after all. Maybe I'm just running away from my life, the same way I used to do back then. And where did I end up? I ended up back here. It kind of makes sense."

Well, in the first fifteen minutes of meeting them, she had gone and made herself vulnerable to the group of rabid teenage girls, which maybe wasn't the best idea.

"So what happens next?" This question came from Keira.

"You're going to hate it," Jane said. "Because we are going to have the welcome ceremony in the gym before dinner. And it's designed to be so embarrassing that you start to drop your guard."

Everyone looked horrified.

"And then at dinner, just don't put your elbows on the table."

"Why not?" Peyton asked.

"Just trust me. Don't put your elbows on the table."

Chapter 4

The opening ceremony was just the way Jane remembered it. Alden was on stage with a microphone, and there was loud music playing when she and the girls walked into the gym. It was like being in a flashback.

What wasn't like the opening ceremony of old was Spencer.

He was standing near the stage wearing . . .

She almost thought she was hallucinating. The beard he'd had when she'd seen him earlier today had been shaved into a mustache. The T-shirt he was wearing was far too tight to be taken seriously, but it was making her think thoughts about his chest and abs that she had no business thinking. And the shorts . . . red, slutty short-shorts that showed off his powerful thighs, and . . .

She had a feeling he was supposed to look like a cheesy coach from an eighties movie. He had a whistle around his neck, and he was wearing a hat with the camp logo on it.

But it wasn't cheesy to her. That was the terrible thing. It was like some hypersexual fantasy, and she couldn't get her mind out of the gutter, in spite of her best efforts.

She needed to get her mind out of the gutter.

How was it that she had just seen Spencer for the first time in years, and he was already taking over her common sense. Her entire brain. Everything.

Absolutely everything.

The gym continued to fill, until all three hundred kids had piled in, along with counselors who seemed familiar to her, and also counselors who didn't.

Alden started to speak, and then the air was split by the sound of three sharp whistling sounds as Spencer stormed the stage making a timeout gesture with his hands.

The kids were glued to the spectacle. Some clearly already bought into the promise of Camp Low Echo, while others were new and horrified by the cringeworthy scene that was unfolding before their eyes.

It was a skit, and in spite of herself, she was laughing. She didn't know whether it was because she was uncomfortable or because she was . . . having an out-of-body experience. But oh, good God, he was gorgeous. And she was being inappropriate, checking him out in this venue. He was a cowboy. Of course, his arms were muscular from all that ranch work. A ranch that he owned. A cowboy wandering around in short-shorts. The display was just gratuitous.

The laughs for the skit were reluctant initially, but eventually everyone was laughing even if it was with embarrassment.

She took in a sharp breath on her own last laugh, and felt as if her lungs were expanding. As if she could take a full breath for the first time in years. She'd forgotten that one of the big gifts of this place was escape.

The isolation that had felt horrible when she was fifteen was the exact thing she'd needed. She'd been cut off from the friends she was trying to impress, from the foster families she wanted to alienate and the biological family she both longed to reconnect with and needed distance from.

She'd been free to be young for the first time in her life.

Not a child forced to adopt the kinds of survival skills more common to a combat veteran than a young girl.

Even now she felt that freedom. She didn't have to try so hard to be a polished, perfect lawyer who didn't betray a hint of her low-class background, who didn't seem like a foster kid, or a foundling, who didn't seem traumatized, or like a success story.

She just felt like Jane.

It was only a coincidence that Spencer was there. Making her laugh, making her feel like someone she hadn't been for a very, very long time.

Someone she'd only ever been for three months at a time. Free, unencumbered by fear and baggage. What she wanted for every kid here was that feeling. An experience that was a luxury other people took for granted. A luxury even she'd forgotten.

Alden put his arm around Spencer. "Spencer Quinn is the longest-standing resident of Camp Low Echo. He started coming here when he was fifteen, and he's been here every summer since. When I'm gone, he'll be your camp director."

Her stomach tightened, and she saw tension around Spencer's mouth, just for a moment.

"If you need anything, if you have questions, Spencer is the one to ask." Alden clapped Spencer on the shoulder. "Now let's all go in for dinner. Your table will have your cabin name on it. You'll be sitting there for the duration of the summer. Let's go eat!"

Counselors tried to lead their kids—Jane included—but it was a thunderous stampede to dinner, with Raccoons One through Six pushing ahead of Pika Four and Chipmunk Two.

She saw the Squirrel Six table right at the center of the room and went straight for it. They were next to Pika Five and Possum Nine.

Spencer was the counselor for Possum Nine.

"Oooh." Aaliyah was looking at the next table. "Not baaaad."

"You're not allowed to be a slut here," Evie said, reaching toward the center of the table and grabbing a roll.

"No one is a slut," Jane said succinctly. "We don't need to shame people."

"Some people need a little shame," Evie said pragmatically.

"No," Jane said. "Life does that to us enough, especially to women. The rules at camp are that we aren't supposed to have physical relationships."

Just as she said that, she sneaked a glance at Spencer and felt her face get hot. They'd broken those rules like champions.

She wouldn't be doing that again.

The camp mess hall had a view of the lake, and there was a large Wheel of Fortune at the front of the room, a wheel with mainly dire consequences. She remembered that wheel from her time at camp. If you were caught with your elbows on the table, or committing any other infractions, you had to spin the wheel of doom and await your fate.

She folded her hands in her lap.

They were served a massive bowl of spaghetti and a giant green salad, and the girls almost collided trying to serve themselves food. She noticed Keira was quiet, watching everyone else dish out the food.

"What is it?" she asked, keeping her voice low.

"Oh, I've never really . . . sat at a table for dinner like this. With other people."

Jane's stomach turned sharply. She'd had dinner with her foster families, but she'd never really felt that she had a family, or anything close to normal relationships.

"Now you have," she whispered.

Keira nodded slowly, then dished her own food.

"GET YOUR ELBOWS OFF THE TABLE, SPENCER QUINN."

The shouting song, led by a teenage boy standing up on a chair, jolted everyone at the table.

"WE HAVE SEEN YOU DO IT TWICE AND IT ISN'T VERY NICE, GET YOUR ELBOWS OFF THE TABLE, SPENCER QUINN."

The people in the room who knew the song joined in, pounding their tables and clapping as Spencer groaned and stood up. Jane knew the song but she was bemused by the fact that Spencer was the main character of the day.

She had a hard time believing the Camp Low Echo pro himself had done this by accident. No, he was setting the expectations for the summer.

She watched as he stood up from his chair—those damned short-shorts—and started to make his way around the table while the singing continued. "ROUND THE TABLES YOU MUST GO."

He wove around the tables while everyone clapped and then made his way to the front of the room. "SPIN THE WHEEL! SPIN THE WHEEL!!"

The campers chanted and pounded the tables, the silverware clattering against glasses and the room shaking as they stomped their feet on the floor. He looked regretful as he stood and spun the wheel, which clicked as it whirled around in a swirl of color.

She watched as it slowed, recalling some of the possibilities.

Mystery Meat—which she remembered being a pretty vile challenge, usually involving some kind of canned meat or a head cheese. Something she would never have known existed if not for camp. Karaoke—which was one of the easier ones, because all you had to do was sing a song. Laps—which just meant jogging around the soccer field. Annoying, but not as bad as some of it.

The pointer landed on Water Slide, to the utter delight of everyone in the room who knew what that meant.

What followed was pandemonium. By design, she knew. Her whole table watched with wide eyes while Spencer made an attempt to escape—which he knew would fail—and other counselors hauled him up over their heads and started to carry him from the room.

"Oh my God, what is happening?" Olivia asked.

"This place is . . ." Nostalgia swept through her as she watched Spencer struggle against his cheerful captors. How could she ever explain this to anyone back in Chicago?

"Well," she said, standing and setting her napkin on the table. "We have to go watch him get thrown down the slide."

"They're going to throw him down the slide in his clothes?" Olivia asked.

"Yes." Suddenly she imagined those particular clothes wet and clinging to his skin, and she felt a little bit warm as she followed the group of people crowd surfing him out of the mess hall.

Her table followed her, if a bit reluctantly, and they all walked out to the massive water slide, which was affectionately known as The Zipper—made from a corrugated black plastic pipe, it shot you down into the water at high speed on a foam mat and made a loud zipper sound as you cruised over the grooves.

Even if you were forced down the slide, you didn't go without a mat. That would just be painful.

Spencer was putting up a big show of resisting even as he was being loaded onto a mat and pushed toward the mouth of the slide, and now even her girls were getting into it. Jane moved closer to the action and found herself in the middle of the fray.

She looked down at Spencer, whose blue eyes met hers, and suddenly she found herself being grabbed by the ankle.

She shrieked as she was pulled down straight into Spencer's arms and onto his strong chest.

Home.

The feeling was undeniable, the word blooming inside her chest as he held her close. She could feel his heart beating against her face, which was pressed against the tightly stretched cotton of his white T-shirt, and she thought she might die.

She was so caught up in the moment that she didn't think at all.

Until she was suddenly plunged into the darkness, that zipping sound echoing in her ears and Spencer's familiar laugh vibrating through her whole body.

That man was taking her down with him.

She'd spent fifteen years avoiding this moment, the perfect metaphor for their relationship.

When she hit the water, she shrieked.

Chapter 5

He hadn't thought. He'd just done it.

Exactly the way he'd lived life prior to being reformed at Camp Low Echo. The last remnant of that part of himself was Jane, so it seemed . . . apt.

A weird thought to have as he careened down a fast-moving waterslide in hot pants, holding the woman of his dirty dreams in his arms.

Life was weird.

That was the last thought he had before he was submerged in the frigid lake water, still clinging tightly to Jane.

He brought them both back up to the surface, and she shrieked like a banshee when they broke the water. "Spencer!"

His name on her lips, on a scream, was a throwback to a moment he didn't need to remember right now. Not holding her like this, and not with an audience.

Arm hooked firmly around her waist, he began to paddle them both the short distance to shore while the onlookers on the hill above cheered their support of his dunking.

He'd gotten it on purpose—it was a great icebreaker.

Dragging Jane into it had been impulsive.

"What the hell, man?" she asked, as they got close enough to shore so they could both stand. She wriggled out of his grasp.

"Opportunity knocked," he said, simply.

"I don't think I deserved that," she huffed, pushing her hair out of her face.

"Oh, I don't think you deserved it either. I just couldn't resist."

Her eyes met his and his stomach went tight. No. No, he didn't need to be going down this road right now. In this stupid outfit with the tight shirt and shorts melded to his body. Though if Jane still had any feelings for him, maybe the clothes would lower her inhibitions.

To what end?

His continual torture, maybe?

She slogged up out of the water, her clothes as pasted down to her body as his own were to his. He couldn't help but admire the shape of her, even though it was already branded into his brain, body and the palms of his hands.

"Cruel," she said, the sand on the shore sticking to her feet as she started to walk toward the path that wound up away from the lake.

He jogged out of the water to keep pace with her.

"Hey, it's camp," he said. "Different rules apply."

"Is that why you have the mustache?" she asked.

That she'd noticed meant something. At least she was taking inventory of his appearance, if nothing else.

"Yes, it is. I try to do whatever I can to disarm the kids as soon as they get here. Hence the elbows on the table, in spite of being very aware of the consequences."

"You just decided to loop me into those consequences."

It felt perilously close to truths they'd been confronting at far too young an age, and things they probably shouldn't be bringing up now.

"Yes, I did."

He left it at that.

"So you really come every summer?" she asked, trudging up the trail.

"I do."

"Why?"

He shrugged. "Alden is the closest thing to actual family that I have. I see him during the rest of the year too. This place means the world to me."

"You're really going to take over when Alden . . . retires?"

"When he dies? Yes. You know he's not going to retire." Just saying that made his chest feel tight, but he didn't see any point in beating around the bush.

"Well, yeah, but I hate thinking about that. Losing Linda was hard enough." A dragonfly buzzed out of the plants on the side of the trail and crossed in front of them both on a dizzy flight toward the lake.

"Yeah," he agreed, his throat constricting.

"That's amazing, though. That you devote so much of your time to camp. I got out. And as far away as possible. One of the kids asked if I was in family law. I . . . I'm not. I'm as far away from all that as I possibly can be. Is that weird?"

He considered her question for a moment. "No. I don't think so. There's a lot of bad stuff out there in the world. I can't blame you for not wanting to be faced with your specific brand of bad all the time."

"Right. That's what it is. I don't want to always sit in this. Though now that I'm here, it feels valuable. This is going to sound stupid, but when I'm in Chicago, it's so easy for me to forget where I'm from. To forget the past and everything else."

He ground his back teeth together. "Oh. Yeah. I haven't forgotten any of it, and I don't think it's because I stayed."

She looked at him, her eyes glistening suddenly, and he knew she was thinking of them. She might never think of him in her daily life out in Chicago, but she was thinking of him now.

They hadn't been each other's first time. Their lives had been so hard, they hadn't been afforded the luxury of the first time being special. Sex had been an escape, a bad decision made under the influence. Even so, they'd been special to each other. Or she'd been to him. Making love to her hadn't been the same as any other time—before or since.

Maybe he wasn't as memorable to her as she was to him.

She'd wrecked him.

Maybe he hadn't returned the favor.

"I couldn't stay," she said.

He felt as if the wind had been knocked out of him. "I know that. I knew it then." He took a sharp breath. "I knew you had a future, Jane, and that it wasn't going to be here in this small town. I knew you were going to go off to school. Good for you."

"It wasn't . . . it wasn't you."

That could be taken two ways, though he knew how she meant it. The other way felt true too. He hadn't been so bad she'd had to leave him, but he hadn't been so good she'd had to stay.

"It's fine, Jane. It was a long time ago. I knew you were going to go. But I think ghosting me might have been kind of unnecessary."

She huffed out a breath. "Oh, you do?"

"I do."

He waited for something. An explanation, denial or insult, but none came.

Instead they reached the top of the hill, and had to smile for their audience and head back to dinner as if nothing had just passed between them. As if he hadn't just gotten so close to breaking through the silence that had haunted him for fifteen years.

One of the boys in his cabin practically leapt onto his back. "Yo! BRO. That was wild."

"Yeah, Manny, bruh, it was super wild," he said, dryly, opting to use slang with him because it made the kids cringe. Anything to break down the barriers between them.

The other boys were jumping irrepressibly, and he looked over at Jane's group. The girls were keeping their distance from the boys while also eyeballing them.

Things really didn't change all that much.

He certainly hadn't changed. He was at summer camp tied up in knots over Jane Cahill. He might as well be fifteen.

They sat back down at their table, where the food was now cold and he was freezing. He should have gone back to the cabin to change, but he was hungry, so a cold butt and cold pasta would have to do.

He looked back over his shoulder, right at Jane, who was looking just as chilly as he was. Well, no, she looked hot. He was truly no better than a teenage boy.

He took a bite of his food and checked in on her again. She was looking at him this time.

If he felt something about that, he chose not to acknowledge it.

He had to survive this whole summer.

The big question was whether he was going to try to get closure on what had happened all those years ago . . . or whether he was finally going to use this summer to let it go.

Chapter 6

Jane was putting on dry clothes in the bathroom when her girls burst into the room, which was filled with other campers getting ready for bed or for campfire, depending on what their evening plans entailed.

Jane was undecided, since she was still recovering from . . . everything.

Particularly how hard his body was. She touched her engagement ring as if it was a talisman that could ward off sexual thoughts.

That was probably not the best way to think of it.

"That was pretty hot," Aaliyah crowed as she approached Jane and gave her a meaningful stare-down. "Getting carried down the slide by a man in booty shorts."

"He's old," Olivia said. "That's problematic."

Aaliyah spread her arms. "Girl, we're problematic or we wouldn't be here."

"No one needs to be problematic," Jane said, even though she wasn't sure that was the correct way to articulate the idea she was trying to convey.

"You're allowed to think he's hot," Olivia said sagely.

Then Jane said another thing she had a feeling she was going to regret. "He's my ex."

The *woooooooo* that rose from the crowd of girls would have made a '90s sitcom make-out scene jealous.

"Oh, no wonder he grabbed you!" Aaliyah said. "Was that inappropriate of him? Should we report him or mace him?"

"No. It's not like that. It wasn't an acrimonious split or anything. We met here. We were campers."

"I thought there was no romance allowed," Evie pointed out.

"There isn't. I didn't say I kept all the rules. But you have to, because now I'm in charge."

"That seems like a double standard," Olivia said.

"It is," she agreed easily. "But I think you'll find that's part of life."

"That doesn't seem fair."

"Life is rarely fair."

"We all know that," Aaliyah said. "It isn't like we're coddled."

"I know," Jane said. "Neither was I. You might not have been coddled, and life might not be fair, but it doesn't mean you can't get where you want to go."

"Are you turning this into an inspirational speech because you don't want to talk about your personal life?" Evie asked.

"I absolutely am," Jane confirmed. "Which you can also do when you're the adult in charge. But one thing that you are right now, is in charge of yourself. I know it doesn't feel that way. I know it feels like all these adults around you are in control. You don't have a say over anything you do. I know that getting into trouble feels like control. Believe me, I know. I've been there. But the problem is, the adults around you don't care. They don't care if you do well, or if you do poorly. Not the people who have set you up to be in the situation that you're in now, whether that's your parents, or the legal system, or your grandparents. You're the one who has to care. You're the one who has to live the life you've been given. You're the one who has to decide what to do about it."

"Right," Aaliyah said. "We can all just become lawyers."

"Not if you don't want to. Become what you want to be. But make a decision about what you want. Give yourself something to grab onto."

"You have everything you want now?" Olivia asked.

She was looking meaningfully at Jane's ring.

"No. I don't know if anybody has everything they want. But I'm not in jail. And I don't have kids that have been taken from me by the state. So I consider myself a winner in that regard. I didn't repeat my mom's cycle. That's something."

"I guess," Olivia said.

"Do you regret leaving him behind?" Aaliyah asked, her dark eyes keen.

"Sometimes I regret that I had to make such a choice. But I couldn't stay here. So I can't regret it."

"I mean, you can," Bella pointed out.

"Yeah. I guess so. But what's the point of that? All any of us can do is the best we can with the facts we have. The fact I had then was that staying with him was a dead end. I needed to go."

"How did you know what you wanted?" This question came from Evie.

"At your age I didn't. The first year at camp was just me figuring out that life didn't have to be so hard all the time. That I could have some fun. And not the kind of fun that is actually kind of painful."

The girls looked like they knew exactly what she meant, and she felt sadness for them.

"I'm going to campfire," she said. "Anyone else?"

A couple of the girls decided to go with her, while the rest decided to stay behind in bed. It had been a long day. A long day of introductions, and re-introductions for Jane. But that was why she wasn't ready to settle in for the night.

Or maybe she just wanted to see Spencer again. Which was dumb. She shouldn't want to see Spencer again.

But part of her would always be that lovelorn teenage girl.

Part of her would always hold a candle for him. But it was easier to do when he wasn't anywhere around.

They approached the fire pit, and she saw him, sitting there wearing gray sweatpants and a white T-shirt, roasting a marshmallow over the flame, the fire casting a glow on his handsome features.

"You like him," Aaliyah said, elbowing her.

"I'm engaged," she said.

"But you aren't dead," she pointed out.

Then the girl walked away from Jane, making a beeline toward one of the boys on Spencer's team. Great. She had a feeling she was going to be breaking up young love at some point. It would be better for Aaliyah, and for that boy, if they just stayed uninvolved with each other, with anyone, while they were this age.

Life was hard enough without adding love to the mix. It was still hard for her to deal with love now.

Did she love? That question nearly stopped her in her tracks. The truth was, she felt more when she looked at Spencer than she ever had looking at Colin. She had convinced herself for a long time that Spencer haunted her because he was tied to teenage feelings. And in her mind, teenage feelings were big. They were uncontrollable. They were part of her past self, which she had left behind long ago.

But now, she wasn't so sure that was the truth of it. Because she wasn't a teenager anymore, and he still made her heart feel like it was going to explode. Looking at him still made her feel like she might die. That wasn't overly dramatic or anything.

Muscle memory carried her to where the marshmallow roasting implements were kept, just as they had been when she was a camper. She grabbed hold of one of the skewers, then picked up a marshmallow and sat down—far away from Spencer. As she began her roasting, she looked up and met his gaze over the flames. Her whole face grew hot. She tried to ignore the intensity of her reaction. She knew that he was going to come over to her before he moved. She could just sense it. Because there were a couple of immutable truths in life. And one was that Spencer Quinn seemed to move closer to her, no matter where they were. If they were close, he was going to get closer. It was who they were. How they were. How they had always been.

He sat down beside her and put his marshmallow back in the fire. She didn't say anything. And neither did he. But she could feel the tension building between them all the same. Could feel years of unspoken words, dreams that she tried to pretend were nothing more than memories, and not a secret longing for a life she'd had to leave behind. She had the sudden, irritating realization that maybe it wasn't only Colin who needed to figure out what he wanted. Maybe she didn't actually know what she wanted. Maybe it wasn't fair to Colin that she was still so attracted to a man she hadn't seen for fifteen years. Maybe it wasn't fair to him that Spencer still had so much of a hold over her. Maybe there were issues in her relationship that she hadn't wanted to identify. That she hadn't wanted to acknowledge. Maybe she didn't have the right to feel quite so outraged that Colin was having doubts. Maybe some of them came from her own behavior. It was kind of a crazy realization to have just because she was sitting next to a man roasting a marshmallow.

So, that said something.

"What kind of lawyer are you?" he asked. Then he laughed. "It's kind of ridiculous that I've touched you everywhere, and I don't know what you do for a living really."

Her breath caught. He was speaking so low that nobody else would be able to hear what he'd said, but she'd heard it. And that was enough. She should scold him. She certainly shouldn't think it was sexy. And she definitely shouldn't answer him. She shouldn't treat what he was saying as a legitimate observation. Damn him.

"I work for a law firm that is colloquially known as the Death Star. It's huge. Basically, we take all kinds of cases. A lot of commercial litigation, a lot of advising for financial institutions and government entities. Mainly, I help collect data, conduct interviews, put massive numbers of legal documents together . . . I'm a glorified paralegal. Which is actually why I'm on a little bit of a break from my job."

"I see," he said, clearly not actually seeing.

"Basically, I'm being kept doing busy work because I'm very good at it. I could be doing more. But if I was promoted, they would have to pay me more, and they don't want to do that."

"Do you want to be promoted?"

She thought about the long hours, the way everyone at the firm wore their stress on their faces, carried it on their shoulders.

"I don't know. There's nothing else to do but continue to work hard and get promotions. Eventually, become a partner. Though, at a place like that, I'm asking for an awful lot."

"You're not getting it," he said.

"No. I haven't been."

"But you want it."

"I said I did."

"I don't believe you."

"Clearly. Or why would you ask me the same question more than once?"

"I know you. You're extremely driven. When your whole heart is in something, it's obvious."

"I hate to break it to you, Spencer. But you haven't known me in fifteen years."

Her statement didn't feel especially fair. Because there were things she still believed she understood about him, even though they hadn't been anywhere near each other for a long time. There were certainly things he knew about her.

It felt uncomfortable even to admit that to herself.

"Okay. Keep telling yourself that."

"I don't have to keep telling myself anything. I haven't thought about you all that much."

"Don't embarrass us by lying."

"I'm not embarrassed."

"That shows a lack of self-awareness."

She scowled at him. "You're extremely cocky—do you know that?"

"Of course I do. I've always known that. It's been true my whole life. It's probably the reason I survived."

She couldn't argue with that. She knew his father had been cruel. Only self-confidence had helped him survive.

She had known it then; she knew it now.

Maybe he knew her too. Which made her feel far too transparent wearing an engagement ring that maybe meant nothing.

"You don't want to do family court," he said.

"No, as I said before. Yet you brought it up again. Does that mean you don't believe my first answer?"

"I do believe it. I just think it's interesting."

"Why? Am I supposed to want to be stuck endlessly in a system that made my life hell? I believe that is what we call a Sisyphean task."

"Maybe *you* call it that. I've never called anything Sisyphean. That word is above my pay grade."

"I don't believe you."

"That's fine. So I'm the only one who's offensive for not believing something?"

"You are deeply obnoxious," she said.

"Noted."

They finished roasting their marshmallows and built s'mores, eating them in silence.

She wasn't sure if she was glad for the quiet or not.

By the time they finished, most everyone else had meandered back toward the cabins. She and Spencer had lingered. It had felt perfectly reasonable at the time. As if they were just roasting marshmallows. But now she thought maybe they had both lingered on purpose.

Now, it felt intentional.

She stood up, brushing some imaginary dirt off the back of her shorts, and began to walk away from the fire pit.

He followed along with her. She should tell him not to. But that would be weird. Weirder than just letting him follow.

She curled her hands into fists. She continued down the trail, and he went along with her. Her heart was pounding so hard, she was almost sure he would be able to hear it. As they went around a slight curve, she was the one who ducked back off the trail, letting the branches of a tree envelop her. He went with her. Suddenly, he was so close she could breathe him in with ease. Touching him would be the easiest thing. Easier than breathing.

Without thinking, she did just that. Without thinking, she put her fingertips against his collarbone. He reached up, grabbed hold of her hand, his palm coming down over the top of her engagement ring.

"One thing we haven't discussed yet," he said. "You engaged?"

"Yes," she whispered.

"Then we don't have anything else to say to each other."

He pulled away from her, and she felt he had taken a piece of her with him.

He hadn't needed to lean in for her to know that if she'd said she wasn't engaged, he would've kissed her. She was angry that he hadn't. Even angrier that he assumed she would've let him kiss her, even though she absolutely would have. Angry that he was assuming they were having a moment, even though she was assuming the same.

Basically, she was outraged, and it wasn't fair. She wanted him, and she shouldn't. She hadn't been nice to him down at the campfire; she wasn't being faithful to Colin; generally speaking, she was a disaster.

Still, she was mad at Spencer.

Fair or not.

"My wedding was postponed," she said.

"Postponed?"

"Yes. He's not sure."

"Oh, he's not."

He put the emphasis on *he*. As if to imply that she was the one who maybe wasn't certain, and given what she had been thinking earlier, maybe he was not wrong. Another thing that she was unfairly annoyed about.

"No. He's not. It's one reason that I'm here. Everything fell apart at once. I got passed over for promotion, and my fiancé decided to delay our wedding."

"So, two things that you don't seem to actually want got away from you. And what? You don't have an excuse anymore to stay where you're at? You decided to come here to test out your old life?"

"No," she said. "That's not it. I'm . . . I'm at a crossroads. And I don't know what to do. You're acting like I've been secretly planning an escape. All of this hit me without any warning."

"No warning?"

"No," she confirmed.

"Because it seems to me that maybe you don't want any of it. You know why I think that?"

"I have a feeling you're going to tell me whether I want you to or not."

"Then I will. I can tell when you want something, Jane Cahill. You're on fire with it when you do. It's why I didn't try to stop you from leaving. It's why I didn't even ask you to stay. Because you burned with the conviction that you needed to go. I didn't know how to leave. Alden and Linda were my only family. Plus, I knew that I would hold you back. I knew that being stuck with me wasn't going to get you a damn thing. I was just going to be a millstone around your neck. I knew that. So I let you go. Because I could see the fire in you. You don't have any fire now. Not when you talk about the job you do. It's like a list of facts. But there's no conviction in your voice. You wouldn't have leaned into me just now if you cared at all about your fiancé, because the Jane Kelly Hill I know loves too deeply to split her affection. To kiss one man while she wants another. Hell, she can't even keep a boyfriend while she heads off to college. Because her feelings are too deep for that. Too big."

"Great," she said. "That's great. You just think you get to psychoanalyze me because what? We had sex fifteen years ago?"

"It wasn't just that, and you know it. Don't cheapen what we had. Don't cheapen it because you're mad at me for calling you out."

"You don't have the right to call me out. You haven't been involved in my life for these past fifteen years. We saw each other for two seconds at a funeral four years ago. We don't know each other."

"I would argue that we do. Maybe better than anyone else in our lives. Because we let our guards down for each other."

"Maybe we did. But I'm not that person anymore. I've changed. Haven't you?"

"I thought maybe I had. But now I wonder. Your being back here, it reminds me too much of who I was. And it feels pretty damn close to the surface. Like I can reach out and touch myself back then. And you too. Maybe neither of us has changed."

"No. I have. I changed because I had to. And that's what I want to teach the girls here. That they can change."

"Then why did you want to kiss me?"

"Because I still think you're hot," she said. She wasn't going to bother denying it. He'd already called her out. What was the point of pretending she hadn't wanted to kiss him?

"Well. That's not enough for me." He shook his head. "Maybe you *have* changed. Because you wouldn't have used me like that back then."

She wanted to say something sharp and cutting. She wanted to deny his accusation.

It wasn't fair. It was the most unkind interpretation of what she was feeling.

But what was the point? She didn't need him to like her. In fact, she just needed him to step away from her. She needed to get her sanity back. Because he was right to have stopped this.

He was.

She turned away and started to walk back up toward the trail. He caught her by the elbow. "I want to make myself really clear—it's not that I wouldn't. Just not while you're wearing that."

Her heart was thundering. She felt . . . undone. She hadn't felt like this in a long time. Well. Not since the last time she had tangled with Spencer Quinn. There was a reason she'd left.

She wasn't the kind of person who could afford *undone*. She couldn't afford to be distracted. She had an uphill climb.

She hadn't been able to afford to bring anyone with her.

And she couldn't afford any disruptions now. Everything was already a disaster.

She didn't need to break her fragile life open with a Spencer Quinn–sized projectile.

No way.

Chapter 7

Maybe he'd overreacted. Just maybe. The rest of the week passed without incident. Unless Jane Cahill's haunting his dreams counted as an incident. To be fair, that wasn't an entirely unusual experience. It was unusual to be haunted by Jane while she was nearby.

He didn't have time for that. He had unruly hooligans to take care of. And they really were testing him. There was a burgeoning romance happening between Jane's girl Aaliyah, and his own Zane. So that was going to be a real problem. He could already tell.

He knew there was no point saying anything. There never was. Kids were going to go ahead and break their own hearts over their hormones every day of the week.

It was a time-honored tradition. One he'd participated in.

One you very nearly participated in again last week.

No. He was a grown man now. He knew what he was doing.

He felt as if he was standing outside himself, watching his own bravado. He wanted to point and laugh at the moron he was for thinking he was somehow more immune to Jane than he had ever been before.

That he was somehow in control of both his libido and his emotional reaction to her.

He looked up, and she was walking toward him. It was about time for the games to begin. Every Saturday, the camp held ridiculous yard games. Today, he was paired up with her. And that meant they were going to have to get along.

Shouldn't be a problem. In theory.

But looking at her almost felt too bright. Too vivid.

Hadn't he learned anything? She was engaged.

Right when she'd first shown up, he'd thought maybe that didn't matter. But he wasn't going to touch her as long as she wore another man's ring. He owed that to his past self. To the boy who had let her walk away without even putting up a fight because he had known it was the best thing for both of them.

Hell. The best thing for her. He wasn't sure it had been good for him at all.

He would've been better off with her.

She could've been his ranch wife.

Just the thought made him want to laugh.

She never would've been happy with that existence. And the real truth was, what he wanted was her happiness. Even at his own expense.

He couldn't exactly say he wanted her to have no regrets. Sometimes, he wished that she regretted not being with him.

But he never wanted to be one of her regrets.

That was one thing he couldn't have withstood.

One thing he couldn't bear.

Yeah. He could deal with a lot of things.

But better to know for sure that whatever Jane Cahill numbered among her regrets, he wasn't one of them.

He'd been good to her.

She'd been good to him.

It was too easy for him to feel wounded by her. To feel scarred by their love affair. But the reality was, there had been bright, shining moments of real caring that hadn't come from anyone else in their lives.

Sure. Part of it had been a physical, hormonal teenage affair. But a good portion of the attraction had been real, deep emotion.

The kind of emotion that had the power to take his breath away.

The kind that hadn't been matched before or since.

No reason to think about that now, while he was looking at her and those hot shorts.

He knew she wasn't immune to him. He wore his own shorts a little bit too short in order to be ridiculous, but he'd seen the way she looked at him.

If he was going to egg her on, he would tease her about those looks. He wasn't going to, though. He was the one who had put a stop to that kiss.

He has cold feet . . .

Of course, she was the one who had come here after so many years away. Had she known he was going to be here? She claimed she didn't. Yet he was here every year.

You just want to believe she knew. You're still that teenage boy with fantasies about marrying her.

God. He didn't know anything about functional families. About marriage.

He'd learned a lot about found family over the last fifteen years. But that wasn't the same. He wouldn't know what to do with a wife. He wouldn't know the first thing about being a father.

And yet part of him still ached when he thought about having a family. Especially with her.

A couple of the other counselors—Deb and Sarah—were running the lawn games, and they proudly proclaimed that it was three-legged race day.

He and Jane looked at each other. They were going to be paired up. That was the way it went. Counselors were always on the same team.

Which meant he got to put his hands on her. Bad news. Also great news.

The Jane Cahill experience.

Aaliyah and Zane quickly paired up, while the other kids chose partners, not necessarily across gender lines. He and Jane looked at each other.

"Didn't we do this once quite a while ago?"

"I seem to recall," she said.

He sure did. Being fifteen, getting paired up with her, putting his arm around her. Oh yeah. He remembered well how excited he'd been about that.

It was one of those indelible memories, burned into his brain like an emblem.

He decided to defuse the situation. He smiled. "I'm not a gangly fifteen-year-old anymore. Probably won't trip us."

"Bad news is," Jane said, "I'm out of practice. I haven't actually run a three-legged race in a long time."

"Funnily enough, it's only been about a year since my last time."

She shook her head. "That's ridiculous."

She looked around the yard. "Who do you normally run it with?"

A spark ignited in his chest. She was jealous. She was jealous of whomever he'd been running three-legged races with. Fair enough. He was jealous of the guy who'd put that ring on her finger. And he would imagine there were any number of people she'd run three-legged races with prior to that. Just like there were any number of women he'd run three-legged races with outside of camp, so to speak.

"A lot of times I'm paired up with Ella. She's not here this year. I've run with Amanda, LaTisha, Cassie, Sara . . . Oh wait, you were just asking about the actual three-legged race."

"Oh, you're a jerk," she said, smacking her hand against his chest, and he fought the urge to grab hold of it and hold it there. They had an audience of kids. He was going to keep it PG. Both for the sake of being appropriate and for his sanity.

"You should be grateful for my experience. It'll work to our advantage."

The look she gave him was flat. "If I recall correctly, it was my experience that really helped out."

He laughed. "Are we still talking about races?"

"Shut up and get the band."

He did, grabbing an elastic band out of the bin, sticking his foot through one side while she stuck her foot through the other. Their bodies were then pressed together as his arm went around her shoulder. She wasn't tiny, but he was tall, and she felt far too familiar pressed up against him. She shouldn't.

As he'd made clear, there had been a whole lot of women since then. The memory of her shouldn't be quite so strong. But it was.

"This is a relay race," he said to the kids. "So we each run a leg of the race."

"Duh," Aaliyah said. "That is literally what a relay is in every context."

"You can start us off then," he said. "Since you're an expert."

She grinned at Zane. "Happy to."

"Jane and I will finish us off."

He looked at Jane, who was staring at him as if she wanted to bite him.

Not in a sexy way. But it would be sexy to him.

"Let's go."

They worked on coordinating their steps all the way to the last position of the relay while the other kids took their various positions.

They stood, hip to hip, side by side.

"If I didn't know better, I'd say this was a plot," she said.

"Maybe it is. Maybe I've been playing the long game. Maybe I coordinated all of this."

"I would be impressed if you had. And frankly, it would be more effort than anyone else has ever gone to for me."

He felt like he'd been sucker-punched. She was trying to keep it light. Make funny comments.

But it wasn't all that funny.

"I'll always swing for the fences where you're concerned, Jane."

And then the sound of the pop gun went off, and the first set of racers took off. "I'm not sure if I'm rooting for her or against her," he said, watching as Aaliyah determinedly strode forward with Zane.

"You have to cheer for her. She's overconfident, and I love that about her."

"Why exactly?"

"Isn't it better that the world hasn't managed to beat that bravado out of her?"

"True and duly noted."

"I thought you were the expert. Given that you've done this every year."

"I can't say that I'm an expert. Every year the kids are different. I mean, quite a few of them come for a whole three-year cycle. But there's still a different dynamic every year. Some kids, they don't come back. Because they really do disappear. Fall off the map." Aaliyah and Zane made it to the next group and tagged their teammates, who took off running. Well, as much running as could be done in a three-legged race.

"That breaks my heart," he said, looking at Jane's profile. At the lovely slope of her nose. The way her dark hair curled around her temples. "Because you wonder if they were just too far gone. Or if there was something you could've done. Something you missed."

"At a certain point everyone has to make their own choices," Jane said. "We did. You know you have to take the help that's offered. And I don't know if it matters whether or not the blame lies with the teens, or with the adults who failed them originally. It's a tragedy either way."

"Yeah," he said, his voice rough.

Their third-wave runners started, then tripped and fell.

They scrambled up as best they could, but thankfully a few other kids fell too.

He supposed that wasn't the best thing, to be thankful that the teenagers were falling down. But he did want to win.

At this point it was a point of pride. He could run a three-legged race backward. With anyone.

Of course, he wasn't running the race with anyone. Or backward. Running with Jane would be a distraction.

And then, he didn't have time to think about it anymore. It was their turn to go. He wrapped his arm around her tightly as her arm secured his waist, and they made their way as quickly as possible down that final strip of grass.

Their legs moved together, carrying them quickly, if awkwardly.

It reminded him far too well of how their bodies worked together in other contexts.

No.

He didn't need this. No. He didn't need it all.

And yet, he wanted it. Was enjoying it on some level.

The warm press of her body against his.

Maybe he could just . . .

They nearly tripped, and he lifted Jane up, propelling them

both forward across the finish line as her legs wiggled helplessly.

"I don't think you're supposed to do this," she howled as they pitched themselves over the line.

"I'm the one that's been here for the last fifteen years. I know the rules."

They were lying there in the grass, pressed together. His heart was beating hard, but not from exertion.

He felt like a kid again.

For better or worse. He felt like a kid, staring down at the most beautiful woman he'd ever seen.

Suddenly, she sat up and freed them with near desperation in her movements.

"Squirrel Six and Possum Nine are the winners!"

Their victory, announced through the megaphone, felt like a secondary thing compared to the thrill of touching Jane.

He really was regressing. All the way back to his teenage self.

For the rest of the week, he managed to keep his distance from her. Most of the time. There were any number of bonfires, dinners and activities where their campers were in close proximity. Breakfast and lunch much the same.

But he didn't go out of his way to approach her. And she kept her distance from him.

"What's the deal with you and the Squirrel Six lady?"

It was Xavier who'd asked that question, and he wanted to punch the kid in the face. But you couldn't do that to your campers. Instead, he gritted his teeth.

"What do you mean?"

"Seems like you like her," he said.

"I *like* her? I'm not in high school," he said. "I don't . . . like anybody."

"You have sexual tension," Zane said.

Spencer gave him a flat look. "I don't think so."

"Nah," he said. "You do."

"Where are you getting that from?"

"You're avoiding her. You don't avoid anybody. You're weirdly friendly. You seem to enjoy talking to every single person you come across, but when you see her, you turn and go the other way. Ever since the three-legged race."

"You know, I think I liked it better when you guys just didn't pay attention to anything."

"We're bored out here," Xavier said. "We don't have anything else to do."

"It's true," another one of the boys chimed in. "We have to make our own entertainment. And you and Jane make good entertainment."

"I don't think that's true."

"You can think whatever you want. But it's pretty obvious."

"Whatever you're sensing . . . it's not about now. She's . . . We dated. Back when we were at camp." There. He would give them that.

"So you have unresolved stuff."

"Oh," he said. "It was resolved. But thank you."

"Hey," Zane said. "I'm a minor. Don't go implying things like that to me."

"Bro," he said. "If you picked up my implication, then you don't need to be protected from it."

The kids snickered. "Just saying. I think you still have a thing for her. And she definitely has a thing for you."

"Does she?" He despised himself for asking that question.

"Aaliyah said she talks about you," Zane said, looking smug. "And that she gets all nervous before we go to campfire and things because you're gonna be there."

"Really?"

"Yeah. Really. That's what I heard."

"Well. Well." He didn't really have anything else to say to that.

"You should see if she's into you," Xavier said.

"She's engaged," he said.

"No one who looks at you that much is all that engaged," Zane muttered.

He carried hope closer to his chest than he should. All through the rest of the day.

The problem was that it wasn't just attraction burning inside him. It was genuine curiosity about her. About her life. Who she was now.

And when he chose to sit next to her at the campfire that night, he told himself it was actually because there was no reason he shouldn't be able to be friends with her. In fact, his conversation with the boys pointed the way to that friendship. Yeah. They'd had something once. She'd moved on. So had he. But the ways in which they had moved on, the shape their lives had taken since then . . . that was something they didn't really know about each other, and it could be interesting to learn.

Hell, it was interesting. They were success stories. He should know everything about her so that he could tell other campers. He was mature enough to see the value in knowing her apart from his attraction. Because he wasn't a teenage boy. No matter how hot and bothered being close to her made him feel.

The minute he sat down beside her and felt the warmth of her body, he questioned his logic.

"Oh," she said, jumping.

"I'm not the boogie man, Jane," he said.

"Oh I know, Spencer," she said, imitating him by using his name. It was weird that he'd tacked her name to the end of his statement. Maybe it was because he missed saying it.

One of the many things he missed, he supposed.

"Well, then you don't have to get jumpy just because I sat down next to you."

"You've been ignoring me."

"I thought you were ignoring me."

She turned to look at him, and he realized his mistake. He couldn't be neutral with her. There was no way. There was no way he was going to be able to make small talk, pretend that he just wanted to be friends.

She was smart, she was amazing. Everything she'd done in all the years since she had left made his heartbreak worth it. Because she'd achieved the success she wanted, and he should be happy that she had found somebody else.

But what he felt for her was just so strong, he couldn't turn it off.

"I'm gonna be real with you," he said. "It felt easier to avoid you because I want you. But I don't need to make that the defining thing between us. I'm interested in you. As a person. Not as a partner. I want to know about every step you've taken since you left here."

Her eyes looked wide, frightened, and she glanced away from him into the fire. "Spencer, I . . ."

"I do have a question though. Why did you come back here? You had to know that I might be here."

"I wasn't thinking about you," she said.

"Ouch," he said.

"I'm not trying to be mean. I didn't think about you because it was too uncomfortable. Okay? I don't think about you. I don't really think about this place. I chose to leave it behind. I see my earlier self as someone totally different from the me I am now. Because it's easier."

"Easier than what?"

"Easier than having to accept the fact that I let go of something I cared about a lot in order to rescue myself."

"I think that's life. We don't get to have everything."

"I guess not," she said. "But I found that really painful when I was eighteen."

"Hell," he said. "I find it really painful now."

"You have a girlfriend, Spencer?"

He shook his head. "I don't really do girlfriends."

"Really?"

"I told you. I run in that three-legged race with a lot of different people."

"Yes, you did say that. But I thought you were just being a jerk."

"I was. I was also being honest. I haven't really been inclined toward relationships since you left."

That was a hard admission. Basically admitting that he'd been really messed up by their relationship. That she'd hurt him so badly.

He didn't explain further. She didn't ask. They both had too much to lose.

"Okay, maybe you didn't think about it, but you did know that I would be here. You had to, on some level."

"I don't know. It felt surprising to see you. Just like it felt surprising to see you at Linda's funeral."

"Why? Because you did such a good job forgetting that I existed?"

"If I say yes, are you going to be angry at me?"

Hell yes. He was going to be very angry. Because he had never forgotten about her. Not for one moment.

"There's no point bringing up the past. You have a ranch. I think that's amazing. How did you get into ranching?"

"It's kind of a boring story."

"Indulge me. Since you came and sat down next to me."

"Okay. I worked for a guy for a number of years, and when he decided to retire, he set me up with a really good payment plan on the property. The end."

"That's amazing."

"I know it's not college or anything like that."

"If you'd wanted to go to college, you would've done it," she said.

Until this moment, he hadn't realized that he felt shame about not continuing his education. As if he wasn't good enough for her because that hadn't been his path. He wondered if she thought the same. A strange resentment rose up within him.

And he regretted it, because Jane had never been one to treat him like that. She'd never been a snob. She never acted superior. His reaction was all tied up in this anger over not being what she needed back then.

In the hurt of not being enough.

"Well. What does your fiancé do?"

"He's a lawyer," she said, looking rueful.

"Of course."

She stared into the fire for a long moment. "I'm not very happy."

The words settled between them.

"You're not?"

She shook her head. "No. I'm doing all the things I told myself I wanted to do. I have all the things I told myself were really important. But they don't bring the satisfaction I thought they would. It's not fair or right of me to feel unhappy, because look at what I've achieved—I have so much. It's just so privileged. I would've hated me back then. A woman who has so much money and lives in a fancy apartment in the city and doesn't think she's happy? Yeah. I would've hated me. But I've just been clinging to this idea of what success is. I don't know . . ."

"You don't have to keep doing it."

"I'm not anything without it."

"That's not true. You're you. With or without success, you're Jane. And you've always been enough."

"Well. We both know that's not true."

"You were always enough for me."

He might as well have taken a knife, cut his chest open and just pulled his heart out and given it to her. God dammit. He was such a sap.

He'd spent so many years being closed down, having sex that didn't mean anything, avoiding relationships, and the minute Jane Cahill came back into his life, he opened up a vein.

It was not a good look.

Her eyes went glassy, and she looked away from him. Affirmations from an old boyfriend probably didn't mean anything to her.

If he had actually been that. It was kind of bold of him to apply that label to their situation. He'd been in love with her. He'd been willing to do whatever he needed to do for her, and he had.

But the truth was, they'd been each other's summer person. They'd both had lives apart from this camp.

Maybe he'd never meant to her what she'd meant to him.

And that was a truth he'd been avoiding for a very long time.

"Well, I'm going to head back."

He stood up, and she stood up with him. He didn't say anything as he headed down the path that carried them away from the fire.

But she was following him closely.

He turned around, and it was just the two of them. On an empty path, shrouded in the darkness. And suddenly, it just didn't seem as if anything else mattered. Not the past, not the future, not the ring on her finger. Suddenly, the only thing that mattered was her, and the feeling that had existed in his chest for all these years.

A feeling that was suddenly so much bigger than he was. Bigger than both of them.

He wrapped his arm around her waist. She gasped, her body drawn up against his.

"I thought you said there was no point in this," she whispered. "Not while I'm wearing a ring."

"You know, suddenly I don't care anymore."

He had done self-denial with her for far too long. If she didn't really care about him, then they could face that truth later. If she thought she was better than he, if this was a mistake, they could deal with it after this.

But right now, he was going to have what he wanted.

So he stopped resisting. He lowered his head, and he kissed her.

Chapter 8

She was drowning. Dying. This was what love, attraction, sex had been in her memory, but never in her actual life, never in her actual bed.

Just his mouth on hers was carrying her to another planet. Another plane of existence.

Spencer Quinn had always been one of a kind.

No man, before him, after him, in college, in law school, not even Colin, had ever matched him.

She'd tried. She'd been convinced that whatever had happened between them had been some trick of her imagination. The creation of a girl who had wanted to be loved with such deep, great force that she had turned the physical side of her relationship with him into some kind of romance novel fantasy charged by her deep need to believe that such a thing could exist.

She'd been convinced that she couldn't experience such intense longing now because she had other things. Because she had stability, and school, degrees, a future.

Because she no longer carried that sort of hunger inside her. She'd been wrong.

This kiss was everything she'd experienced with Spencer before, and more.

His mouth on hers was a revelation. A window into not just another time, but into a part of herself that she had shut down, given away.

Spencer.

"I need . . ." His voice was rough—it reflected the desperation she felt.

"Shed," she said.

He knew exactly which shed she meant.

The first time they'd had sex, it had been in there.

They'd waited until their last summer before taking it that far.

So weird that they'd waited so long.

She had lost her virginity far too early, to a boy she barely remembered, who didn't care about her.

After she'd met Spencer, after they'd gotten romantic their second summer, there hadn't been anyone else.

And then they'd waited until the end of their last summer at camp to consummate their relationship. After months of desperate make-out sessions and other activities. Maybe because he had felt special.

It had felt like her real first time.

He still did.

He stood away from her, breathing hard.

He was so beautiful.

She was . . . she was way too good at compartmentalizing things so she didn't feel. So that she didn't feel the intensity with which she missed him, with which she missed this place. This feeling. The need that existed between them. She had let herself be half a person for so long.

Not necessarily because he was her other half, but because she had shut off passion and hadn't even realized it.

Because she believed, somewhere deep inside herself, that she just couldn't have everything.

Who could?

It was a deeply held belief that she'd never truly looked at before.

She had enough. She couldn't have wild, unrestrained passion while also escaping the cycle of drug addiction, poverty, teen pregnancy.

No. Of course not. It was as if she'd been punishing herself in some way.

No. You couldn't have him. Because he was all-consuming. Just have him now.

Yes. It didn't have to be forever. It could just be now. Just a taste. A taste before she went back to her real life.

That life you're not happy with?

She couldn't blow everything up just because she had kissed Spencer once.

Well. She could admit that that kiss had maybe counted as more than one.

"Come on," he said.

He took her hand, and with her heart pounding hard, they rushed through the bushes. She felt like a kid again. In a good way. She hadn't thought there was a good way to feel like a kid.

Not in her experience.

But right now, it felt good.

She felt wild. Reckless. She hadn't been either in so long.

She had thought she had to give away that part of herself. The part that felt giddy joy, that felt excitement like this.

They reached the shed quickly, and she had to laugh when he opened the door and shut them both inside.

"This is insane," she said.

And it was. It had been then. Getting intimate in a garden shed that had any number of creepy crawlies in it, had seemed dangerous and hot back then.

It did right now.

At the realization, she nearly laughed with wild, reckless joy.

She hadn't just missed Spencer. She'd missed herself.

She'd turned that teenage version of herself into an enemy, almost. Something forbidden that she wasn't allowed to revisit or even like. Because she needed to get serious, turn her life around and all that.

But there had been beautiful things about that girl.

This feeling was one of them—the capacity for happiness, for joy.

To experience it now, inside herself, when she hadn't for so long, was quite simply the most beautiful thing she hadn't known she needed.

He cupped the back of her head and drew her in for another kiss. She was lost in it instantly.

It might've been fifteen years ago, might've been now. It might've gone on for only a few minutes; it might've gone on for hours.

And then suddenly, the door opened. And two other people tumbled inside. "Occupied," Spencer growled.

The two other humans scrambled out.

It was Zane and Aaliyah.

"Oh . . ." Spencer rubbed his hand down his face. "Are you kidding me?"

"Coach?"

"This is your fault, man. You told me to go for it," Spencer growled.

"You told him to go for it?" Jane asked.

"Well . . . we knew that he liked you," Zane said, sheepish.

She didn't want to deal with this. She wanted to continue to be in a passionate haze. She wanted to continue to get the thing she really wanted.

But she was going to have to be the Squirrel Six counselor and enforce the rules.

"You are breaking the rules too," Aaliyah said, way too fast.

Jane glared at her.

"We are adults," she said.

"Fornicating around impressionable youths," Aaliyah pointed out.

"The impressionable youths were supposed to be in bed." Jane stared at her. "And were definitely not supposed to be in here with a boy."

"Why was I able to escape? You weren't supervising us."

"It's not curfew yet," Jane said.

"Okay," Spencer said. "We don't need to argue over this. No one's getting in trouble. But you two are on notice."

"What the hell?" Zane asked.

"You're fifteen," Spencer said. "And it would be irresponsible of me to look the other way while you guys get up to whatever you're getting up to. Be sneakier. We were."

"We caught you," Zane pointed out.

"But no one caught us back then. So get good, or stop trying to break the rules."

They all looked at each other. "In the meantime," he said, "no one needs to go being a court reporter."

He kept on staring at them. "Go on. Get."

"Fine," Zane said.

"We're both going back in five minutes. If you're not in your cabins, we're sending out a search party."

They moved reluctantly away from the shed, and Spencer closed the door, then hit his head against it twice. "Oh, why is this my life?"

"It's probably for the best," she said, her voice shaking just as much as her legs were.

"For the best of what?" he growled. "Certainly not my physical well-being."

"I just mean . . . I don't know."

He moved to her and cupped her face. "Don't run away from me."

"We are being hypocrites," she said.

"No, we're not. We're adults. They are kids. And they could get themselves in trouble."

"Just like us?"

"Just like us. But I meant what I said. If you're going to go breaking the rules, you have to earn it. You have to be a little bit cleverer than we were."

"We should've hung a tie on the door."

"Why would anyone have a tie?"

"It's just what we did in law school."

"Right. Anyway."

It seemed she'd hurt his feelings mentioning that. She put her hand on his face. "I'm sure you had a place to yourself and didn't have to warn roommates when you brought women back."

She wanted to remind him that he'd made it clear there had been others.

"Yeah. True." He took a deep breath. "Barn Owl is empty."

Barn Owl wasn't part of a series of cabins like the rest of them. There was only one. It had been the caretaker's lodging, but she knew where it was.

"Okay . . ."

"Meet me there. Tonight. After everybody goes to sleep."

"I can't do that . . ."

"Please. But if you don't, then . . . I get it."

Her mind was spinning. With exactly what it was he would infer from her absence. *Take a risk, Jane.*

"I'll see."

She walked out of the shed and trudged back to her cabin. She had two options. She could act as if nothing had happened, or she could act as if everything had changed.

That terrified her. She been so certain of who she was, of

what she wanted for so long; the logical part of herself would say that giving it all up for her high school summer love was a foolish thing to do.

But she also missed foolishness.

She sighed heavily and walked back to Squirrel Six. Aaliyah was lingering outside the cabin.

"Sorry," Jane said. "But you know we can't just let you do that."

Aaliyah's arms were crossed, her eyes glittering with tears of outrage.

"I really like him," she said.

"I know you do. And listen, I understand. I do. But I'm also supposed to be the responsible adult, and I can't let you break the rules. I can't let you put yourself at risk."

"But *you* were."

"As Spencer already pointed out, we are adults."

"But you did have sex with him. When you were younger."

"We were eighteen," she said.

"You were a virgin when you were eighteen?"

"No. But he was a big deal. And it felt like the right thing to wait for him. But I couldn't have him, Aaliyah. My future was never going to be with him. So all I did was hurt myself. All I did was hurt my own feelings."

It was exactly what she was doing now, in all honesty. She had a life back in Chicago. Even if she had realized that it wasn't happy, that didn't mean she could just leave it. It didn't mean she could blow it all up. She'd spent years cultivating a life that was more and better than her mother's. Than the life of the father she'd never even known.

She couldn't just stop all that now.

For Spencer.

Because you couldn't put your trust in people. That was the problem. It was a good thing she wasn't wildly in love with Colin. She could admit that. When she got back to Chicago, she was going to have to break up with him. The truth was, his postponing the wedding had really upset her, but it hadn't destabilized her. Because she wasn't wildly in love with him.

She hadn't wanted to be, honestly. Tonight she had realized that she had chosen not to feel those things. Because she had fixed a lot of the external things in her life, but there were still deep emotional wounds that were just . . . there. For her, depending on another person . . . that was foolishness. It was insanity.

She knew why she'd made the decisions she had, but standing there now, she could also appreciate that they'd led her somewhere she didn't want to be.

"I'm just worried for you," she said to Aaliyah. "Not just as a counselor, but as somebody who really, really jumped in with both feet when I was young. I hurt myself badly. Because I knew that I had to leave Spencer. I had to follow my dreams where they took me. And that was away from him."

"I'm not looking for forever," Aaliyah said. "But . . ."

"I know. I'm being a ridiculous adult, telling you not to have feelings unless you know all the consequences, but look how badly we've both been hurt by adults who . . ."

"You're afraid I might get pregnant?"

"Yeah, that's one of the things I'm afraid of. It would be better if you didn't find yourself in that situation, Aaliyah. You've been through enough. You are so smart. I can tell. And just . . . brave, and wickedly funny. I have enjoyed getting to know you so much. Whatever you want to be, you can be."

"How do you know that?"

"Because I just do. Here's my pledge to you, right now. I'll pay for your college education."

"What?"

"I'll pay for your college. Whatever you want to do, Aaliyah. I'm a lawyer. I make a lot of money. I can afford it."

"Why would you offer to do that? You don't even really know me."

"I see myself in you."

"Let me guess. You'll only pay for my school if I don't mess around with Zane."

"No. You don't have to meet some invisible standard either. I just want you to know that you have a future, so you'll take it seriously as you make decisions."

"You're kidding, right?"

"I'm not."

"But I still have three years of high school left. And I keep getting bounced around different foster homes . . ."

"Okay. Then let's talk about solutions. We have the summer to figure it all out."

What she really wanted to do was offer Aaliyah a place to live. But she knew the problem was more complicated than that.

Though perhaps it wasn't so complicated. Not with a girl like Aaliyah who was in a difficult place.

The idea of upending her stability like that . . . It scared her. And it stopped her short.

She could promise money. She could promise that easily.

Anything else . . .

Well, all the emotional stuff of dealing with another person was what really felt challenging.

And that included the emotional stuff with Spencer.

"I want to be a lawyer," Aaliyah said.

"You don't have to be."

"Why did you choose to be a lawyer?"

"I knew I would make money in that profession. I knew that people think lawyers are smart. Also, I love to argue, and people used to tell me that meant I would make a good lawyer. Funny story, I'm not sure that's true. I'm not sure you need to be inherently argumentative."

"Oh."

"Yeah. I don't know, major in philosophy if you want to."

"I want to be a lawyer. I want to make money."

"Well. That's how you end up being a lawyer. Just so you know."

"I . . . I dunno what to say. I don't really trust you. Because this is kind of a crazy thing to offer somebody."

"The chance for a future? It shouldn't actually be crazy."

"But no one in my life has ever cared."

"People should care. About their own kids, obviously. But about girls like us. Who are just . . . going to have all of their intelligence wasted because no one in their lives could step up and love them the way they deserved."

"I'll think about it," Aaliyah said.

"Good. I'm not going to make you write me an essay or anything, on what you want to be when you grow up. But maybe let's have a conversation in a couple weeks."

"Okay."

She felt guilty, going into the cabin with Aaliyah, pretending to get ready for bed. She waited until all the girls were asleep.

And then she crept back out of her bed.

She was on the cusp of something. Of some real change. Of really accepting that she needed to change her life. But she was still holding back. She was afraid.

She knew it. She could feel herself hesitating. Even when she'd been out there with Aaliyah. Stopping herself from offering what she really wanted to give that girl.

A place to live. A family.

It was crazy. She had given up so much to avoid teen pregnancy, so that she wouldn't have a daughter Aaliyah's age, and now she was considering . . .

But she cut herself off from so many feelings. And now she felt as if they were all coming out. Rising to the surface.

Maybe it was this place. Maybe it was Spencer. Maybe it was just her, coming to the end of a long road. A road on which she'd told herself that success equated to happiness.

That money, education, proving people wrong, were adequate substitutes for the thrill of actually living.

Her breath froze in her chest, and she put her hand over her heart as she scurried away from the cabin and headed toward Barn Owl.

For one paralyzing moment, she wondered if he would even be there. Maybe he wouldn't come, would think better of it.

But as she stood on the path catching her breath, she knew that wasn't true. Spencer had never let her down.

Spencer had . . .

She'd always believed that he'd let her go away to school because he hadn't really cared about her all that much.

But everything he'd shown her this summer was that he cared a great deal.

And she was suddenly in awe of what might've been a very real sacrifice on his part.

He'd never made her feel bad for leaving.

He'd never asked her to stay. Never once pressured her.

And it was such a strange thing, because she was a girl who had wanted to be loved deeply. His begging her to stay would've made her feel that, she supposed.

But she would've been angry at him too. He truly would never have been able to win with her.

This was what really scared her for Aaliyah. For Zane. Caring so much about somebody as a teen was holding a loaded weapon without really knowing what you were doing.

Hell, it felt that way even now.

It really did.

On a deep breath, she pushed the cabin door open.

There he was. He was barefoot, sitting on the edge of the bed, wearing nothing but a pair of blue jeans.

Oh, she had not been prepared for this. For the glory of adult Spencer Quinn.

She'd seen him with his shorts and T-shirt plastered to his body, but this was different.

All that beautiful, golden skin on display. His muscular body revealed to her.

He had been beautiful when he was eighteen. But he was all man now. And incredible.

"Oh, I'm really glad that I came," she said.

"I'm glad you did too."

How was it possible that she felt so much for him? This overflow. How was it that it felt as if so much time had passed, but also none at all?

How was it that she felt like an entirely different person, and so painfully the very same one?

She had to put it down to the mystical magic of the two of them.

Maybe she had to stop trying to make sense of something that was better off felt, not thought about.

She moved close to him, and he wrapped his arm around her waist. She looked down at him, pressing her hands against his bare chest. Her palms burned, and she could feel his heart raging beneath her touch.

"Spencer," she whispered.

"I never got to have you in a bed. It was just that furtive time in the shed, and then down at the water, do you remember?"

"'Course I remember. It was crazy stupid, and we didn't use a condom."

"You were on the pill," he pointed out.

"I know. But common sense would definitely say that you should double up."

"We didn't have a lot of common sense with each other."

"No. We didn't. And it scared me."

I'm still scared.

She didn't say it. But she didn't have to. He pulled her onto his lap, brushed his knuckles down the side of her face. "And now?"

She figured that she would answer by asking him a question instead.

"You've always been the most beautiful man I've ever seen, do you know that?"

"You are such a silly girl," he said.

Then he reached up, pulled her face down to his and kissed her. The kiss was deep and long. And no one was there to interrupt them now. The cabin was secluded, with only one light on. They had a comfortable bed. *Ours.* It suddenly felt like too much and not enough all at once. She felt as if she was standing on the edge of a precipice. And she resented that. Because it was as if her whole life had been made up of big decisions that she couldn't afford to ever get wrong. As if there were impossibly high stakes, and one wrong move would ruin everything forever.

It had been easier to walk away from him than try to figure out how to deal with the kind of passion that flared up between the two of them. With such intensity of emotion.

But now, she was a well-off lawyer. She had all the things. So she could take the risk. Surely.

She was the one with the power. With control. Because after all, education and money were the keys to so many things—hadn't that come up tonight in her conversation with Aaliyah? By offering to pay for college, she was offering the teen a chance at a future that didn't have limits.

The ability to make choices. And she had meant what she'd said to Spencer. He wasn't less because he hadn't gone to school.

But if certain things weren't automatically closed off to you, what decisions would you make?

She had been avoiding asking herself that for a very long time. She no longer had all the excuses she'd once had.

So without all those excuses, without school looming in front of her, without fear over her own ability to survive, to make money . . . what would she choose?

Right now, she would choose to kiss him. And keep on kissing him.

He laid her down on the bed, so impossibly hot and hard on top of her.

He stripped her T-shirt away from her body, and she gasped.

She hadn't been with anyone new for a while. Except, he wasn't new. He was Spencer. And that was somehow even scarier.

Then she couldn't think. He was the only one who had ever been able to turn her brain off. It was one of the things that was so scary about him. Because her brain protected her from so many things.

But not this.

She was being baptized in fire, in sensation. His big hands moved over her body, deftly stripping her bra away.

His palms moved over her curves reverently, skimming her nipples, moving down her waist. He unsnapped her shorts, pulled them away from her body, and she sucked in a sharp breath when he pushed his hand down beneath the waistband of her panties, finding her slick and ready for him between her thighs.

She closed her eyes, let her head fall back, let him touch her.

He was so good at this. He knew her body better than she knew it.

Even when they were younger, he'd managed to make her feel things that no one else had.

It was still that way. Like he was magic, or maybe they were together.

Like they were something special that nothing else had ever been. Nothing else ever would be.

He stroked her until she was whimpering. Until she was so close to the edge. She moved away from him, slipping up the mattress, and he grabbed hold of her underwear, tugging it off as she escaped him.

She went up on her knees, just as he got onto the bed, and she reversed their positions so that she was straddling him, naked, the denim rough underneath her rear. She undid the snap on his pants, lowered the zipper. His head fell back, a pained sound on his lips as she rolled her hips back and forth, teasing them both, his hard length pulsing between her thighs.

"You're so beautiful," she whispered.

"I think I'm the one who's supposed to say that," he said through gritted teeth.

"I get to say it," she said, "because I think it."

She reached up, took the ring off her left hand, and set it on the nightstand. "I don't need this anymore."

"I thought you weren't sure."

"I'm not sure about a lot of things, Spencer, but I'm absolutely certain that I'm not marrying Colin. I can't feel for you what I feel and marry somebody else."

"You would have," he said, reaching up and gripping her chin.

"Yes. Because I let myself forget what I feel for you."

Her chest ached, her shoulders hitched on a sob. "I let myself forget because it was too painful. But I think you're right. I think I did know that you would be here. On some level, I think I hoped so. Because we needed to have this chance."

For what, she still wasn't sure.

Or maybe she was. And she was just still denying it.

He reached up and gripped the back of her head, brought her to him for a kiss. She tugged his jeans down, kissing him as they both worked the fabric away from his body. He kicked his pants and his underwear off to the side, and he was gloriously naked.

He reached over to the nightstand and took some condoms out of the drawer.

She pulled away from him. "Is this where you hook up with other counselors?"

"Not for a while," he said.

"Spencer . . ."

"No one's like you. No one. I need to make that really clear to you. You were engaged to somebody else, so don't get mad at me for . . ."

"I'm not," she said. "I'm not. It's horribly unfair. I know it is. Because I left you. I left you, but I wanted you to beg me to stay, and I wouldn't have stayed. I want to be special, and I don't deserve that."

"You're special," he growled, holding her face, bringing her forehead down to his. "Don't you know that you are the only woman I have ever loved? I can't forget you, Jane. I've never been able to. You broke my heart. And I never wanted to give it to another person. I'm not even mad that you broke my heart. Because it was an honor. To have loved you that much. I'm proud of you. Everything that you are. Everything that you've become. You couldn't have done it with me. Hell, I know I wouldn't have helped you."

"It's not true. You did help me. I can actually never know what my life would've been like without you in it. You cared about me in a way that nobody else did. The way you cared about me made me see value in myself that I didn't see before. I don't think I could have done it without you. I don't think I would have tried."

He kissed her. Deep and long. With all of the feeling she hadn't experienced in so many years.

Then he protected them both and thrust up inside her.

She gasped. At the intensity of it. The depth of it.

He was everything. So was this. So were they.

Spencer.

She wanted to cry. Even as she wanted to cry out her pleasure.

What had ever been like this? Nothing.

They'd been way too young to find each other. And yet. If she had never loved Spencer Quinn when she was a teenage girl, she might not have loved herself enough to become what she was now.

So what do I do now?

She didn't have the answer. So she clung to him. As he thrust deep within her. As the desire and pleasure built between them.

Spencer.

This man who had loved her when he was a kid loved by no one. When she wasn't a lawyer. When she wasn't anything.

This man who was . . . He was still here. At this camp. Giving all of himself, not because he couldn't have been whatever he wanted, but because giving back was what he wanted. Because being here for these kids was what he wanted.

He was more than a good man. He was the best man.

And he made her a deeper, more passionate, more vibrant and alive version of herself.

As the pleasure built inside her, as she couldn't hold back her climax anymore, she felt a wave of certainty wash over her. She had never stopped loving him.

She'd just turned off that part of herself because she had been filled with too many conflicting emotions.

And right then she accepted something for the very first time. She could have stayed with him just fine.

She wouldn't have had as much money. Maybe she wouldn't have reached her full professional potential, but she never would have become her mother. Just as he would never have become his father. There was no question about that. He was just good. He cared. About people more than he cared about himself. There were so many different ways to live a good life.

There had never been only one path for her.

But she had made it. She would never have any question about whether or not she could succeed.

She was grateful for that.

As her pleasure crashed down over her, as she cried out his name. And she knew that she was ready to make a different choice.

He gathered her in his arms, breathing hard as her head rested against his chest. And before she could say anything, he spoke.

"Stay with me. Or let me go back with you. But don't give us up again."

Chapter 9

It was the strangest thing, because he hadn't let himself beg her to stay back then. He'd told himself it was because he respected her dreams. Wanted her to have what she wanted, and that was true. To a degree. Another part of it was that he hadn't believed he was worthy of her. Not really. Hadn't thought he was good enough to ask someone to stay with him. He'd feared he didn't have enough to offer. And that was a holdover from a childhood that had done terrible damage to him.

But he loved her. And he thought he loved her pretty damned well. He could and would give her the life she deserved. Not just financially. But emotionally. Because he loved her. With a depth of passion that he had never felt for anyone else. A depth of passion that had stood the test of time. No, they hadn't walked every step they'd taken since camp together, but she was still Jane. And he still wanted to share his life with her, and what could be a bigger test than all this time and distance, and finding that their love was still the same, stronger even. Sharper. More certain.

This time he was going to ask. This time he would beg.

Because they both deserved the happiness they could have together. "I love you," he said. "I kept myself from begging you to stay with me back then, but not because I didn't love you enough. I just didn't love myself enough. To risk it.

"I want to marry you. Because there's never been anyone else for me. I want to have kids with you. I've been a surrogate dad to a hundred teenagers. I'd like to have some kids. But I could only ever see that happening with you. So it's a dream that I let go of. I want to have a house that's filled with the kind of love you and I never had, but that I know we are capable of creating together. And if I need to go to Chicago to do it, if I need to give up Oregon and ranching and all the things I used to think were important, then I'm going to do it, Jane."

"But the camp," she said. "You're supposed to take over and . . ."

"Yeah. And it'll be hard to tell Alden that I can't do it. But I will. For you. And he'll understand. Because he loved Linda like that. He did."

Suddenly, he heard a rattling sound. A dragonfly had flown into the cabin, attracted by the light.

Jane looked at it, her eyes full of wonder. "I'm supposed to be here," she said. She looked at him with an expression of awe on her face. "I've suspected that. Since I came back. I . . . The dragonfly confirms it. I . . . I don't know how to explain it. But I feel like it's Linda. Sending me a sign that I'm supposed to be here."

"I really hope that's not Linda. Because I don't need her to have seen what just happened."

Jane laughed. "I don't mean like that. I just mean . . . It feels like a sign from her. From the universe." A tear rolled down her cheek and she wiped it away. "I knew I needed to change things. Everything. But that change is at odds with the life I've made for myself in Chicago. And also how much I . . . I didn't want to need you, Spencer. Because needing another person terrifies me. But I do need you. Really. I'm done with Chicago. I'm done with that law firm. I'm glad I didn't get what I thought I wanted."

"And what do you think you'll do instead?"

"Marry you. And start a practice here."

"You're not going to make nearly as much money here."

"I know. I know. And that's going to be a little bit of a problem because I've promised to pay for Aaliyah's college."

He let out a shocked laughed. "Oh. Well. You might want to help her get some scholarships."

"Yes. But . . . she's going to need stability for that." She suddenly looked determined. "We have to adopt her."

"Okay."

"Just like that?"

"I'll give you whatever you want. I don't know if I can possibly make that more clear. And you haven't even told me that you love me."

She looked shocked. Shaken by that realization. "Sorry. I do. I love you. I thought maybe telling you that I was giving everything up and moving here indicated that."

"No. You have to say it. And keep on saying it. Because I don't take it for granted. I can't."

"I love you, Spencer. How can I not? Look at the man you are. The way you give back, constantly. I was too scared to do that. It made me feel too vulnerable. And you've just been out here, being that vulnerable. I've been running. I can't regret going to law school. I don't regret being a lawyer. I like being a lawyer. I do. But I regret not trying to make it work with you long distance. Or asking you to go with me. Any of the hundred things I could've done."

"There's no room for regret. We're here now. We have each other now. Maybe we would have blown it all up then. Maybe we needed to get here. Maybe you needed to almost marry the wrong guy."

"Maybe." She laughed. "Will you really be okay with adopting Aaliyah?"

"You know, part of me knew that I would probably end up doing that someday. It's been an easy thing for me to just care about these kids during the summer. But . . ."

"It's part of your heart."

"Yeah. It's part of my heart. Just like you."

"We just needed one more summer."

"And now we have all the summers after."

He held her close. And this time, he wasn't planning on ever letting go.

Epilogue

Aaliyah was formally adopted before the following summer. After dealing with suspicion, fear of abandonment, and a host of other things that no one could blame her for feeling, she finally had a stable home life with parents who loved her.

And thankfully, she did get a whole bunch of scholarships, because when she decided that what she really wanted was to be a doctor, Jane and Spencer were staring down a whole lot more school than they'd bargained for.

They were just so proud, it didn't really matter.

And Aaliyah credited them with her own mission to inspire Zane to get himself in school. The two of them managed to maintain a long distance relationship until they were able to get married just as she started her residency.

It was a funny thing, being the mother of the bride at just forty-two, and they had three other kids who kept them young, along with three other adopted children who'd come to them at various stages of their teenage years.

Thankfully, Alden was still running camp. But soon they would be doing it. They were ready.

She'd ended up going into family law. Not exclusively. But she'd taken on pro bono work when there were people who really needed help navigating a system that she had often found cruel and unforgiving. She did her best to help people achieve the best outcome possible.

And when she came home at night, she had her family. It turned out that the answer she had been searching for was at Camp Low Echo.

Because that's where her heart had been all along.

The answer was love.

As she walked up the steps to her front porch after a long day of work, her husband walked out the front door, cowboy hat on his head, his tight white T-shirt making her melt all these years later.

"Welcome home, stranger," he said.

She went into his arms and kissed him. After being apart for so many years, she was still amazed that they never had to be apart anymore.

Now they were each other's home.

Forever and always.

Just as they parted, a dragonfly came and landed right on the edge of the porch light.

They both smiled.

Don't miss the final novel in the
Rustler Mountain quartet, *Christmas Valley*.

Chapter 1

Redemption is for men who care. I lost all that a long time ago.

—Butch Hancock's diary, June 15, 1867

Cassidy Wilder had known exactly what she wanted since she was nine years old. To have in this order: a home of her own, a place in the town of Rustler Mountain, and to marry Dalton Wade.

She now had a small home on her brother's ranch—not quite what she was after, but something adjacent. Her brother Austin had turned the tide of public opinion on the reputation of their outlaw family over the last couple of years—which again, wasn't her doing but had given her a sense of belonging she'd been missing.

So really all that was left was marrying Dalton.

The issue was that she might die a vestal virgin waiting for him to ever kiss her.

Dalton was her brother Flynn's best friend, and she knew he was being respectful by not making a move on her. He was being a good friend, a good . . . well, whatever he was to her. Because he was a good guy, and he probably had that weird, wrong-headed idea that sex would corrupt her.

Well, she wouldn't say no to some corruption, but it was becoming clearer and clearer to her that she was going to have to make the first move.

And what better time than now? This season.

The season.

Fa-la-la-la fuck me please, cowboy.

That little internal thought made her shiver, just slightly. Whether because she was pondering the meaning of the word, or because she was afraid she'd be struck by a falling Christmas tree for being so irreverent around a holy season, she wasn't sure.

But the season was upon them, nonetheless.

Rustler Mountain was definitely beginning to look like winter was approaching. The trees in front of the town hall had all turned a vibrant red and orange, and Cassidy knew that meant the leaves would wither and drop by next week. The color was vivid, but fleeting, a metaphor, probably, for something she had never experienced.

Every weekend between now and Christmas, there would be festivities on the main street of town. While Cassidy didn't like to betray the fact that she was secretly soft, in her own heart she could admit it. She loved the decorations, the music, the food. Sometimes she thought that if she could immerse herself in Rustler Mountain Christmas, then she would forget all the Christmases that came before, and most crucially, the Christmas when her mother left her stranded on Austin's doorstep, making her a Christmas foundling at the mercy of three older half brothers who had never even known of her existence.

It would not be surprising if she hated Christmas. For a while it had been difficult. But Christmas in Florida had been different. The way the seasons changed—and they did change, contrary to what people who didn't live there believed—was different from the way they changed in Oregon. The air tasted different, the foliage behaved in a different manner. The way fall turned things crisp before winter made the landscape an easily shattered pane of ice was something she had never experienced until she moved here. Christmas had become a new tradition that had new meaning.

Now it reminded her of how lucky she was to have her older brothers. How lucky she was to have this place to call home. And really, how lucky she was to have Dalton. Her entire family was helping with her future sister-in-law's booth. Jessie Jane was doing blacksmithing demonstrations in a station by the courthouse and answering people's questions and concerns as Rustler Mountain's future mayor. Her term would begin in January.

Cassidy was walking toward the booth now, hands in her pockets, a scarf wrapped tightly around her neck to keep the chill at bay. She could hear music, laughter, conversation, could smell cinnamon, apples and cloves on the air.

There were carolers walking toward her, wearing Victorian costumes, the men in top hats, the women in dark, high-collared dresses with bustled skirts. It was a familiar scene, and yet always different. Always a spectacle.

She quickened her pace as she moved toward the family booth, crossing the street while traffic stopped for her. She waved cheerily at the cars and kept on going.

There was a crowd around Jessie's booth, so she could barely see what was happening, though she could see sparks flying upward and people clapping.

She could see Austin, wearing a black cowboy hat, holding his daughter. And his wife, Millie, standing beside him holding his arm. The sight made Cassidy ache, but not in a bad way.

One of the things that Cassidy was having a difficult time wrapping her head around was how different everything was this Christmas.

A couple of years ago Austin and Millie got married; then they had a baby. Then Carson married his best friend Perry, and now Flynn and Jessie Jane were engaged after what seemed to Cassidy to be a whirlwind fling.

She couldn't imagine anything like that.

Because Dalton wasn't a whirlwind.

He was stable and steady. He was everything she valued.

Right. All of the women he'd had casual affairs with would call him stable and steady.

Okay. Maybe they wouldn't.

But she knew him as stable and steady. He was always good to her. Always patient and wonderful and exceptionally kind.

He was everything she could ever want in a man.

The crowd around the booth began to disperse, and that was when she saw him.

Hands moving in broad gestures as he told a story that made Jessie and Perry double over with laughter. Cassidy felt an absurd prick of jealousy. She had nothing to be jealous about. Perry and Jessie weren't single.

She picked up her pace. She cut across the lawn rather than walking around the perimeter and ignored the delicious-smelling treats as she made a beeline for her family.

"Hi," she said.

The conversation broke off, and she became very aware of the fact that she had just crashed in. Not only that, but they had all responded to her appearance by ceasing their conversation.

Her brothers were careful with her. Maybe a little bit too careful, because of the circumstances surrounding her coming to Rustler Mountain. Everyone was so painfully aware of the fact that she'd been abandoned, and while it was really sweet that they worried about her and all, she didn't need to be treated like a charity case. Or like she was tragic.

Though, to be fair, she definitely acted like the youngest, most coddled member of the group. It was a learned habit. And now that everybody was pairing off, getting married, having children, it seemed . . . silly. She felt silly. She wanted things to change.

She looked at Dalton, and her heart jumped. "What's so funny?"

"Oh, I was talking about the time my brother and I were hunting and he got a deer. Then we came up over the mountain, and there was a bear feeding on the deer that he just dropped. Well, then he got the bear, and went running down the hill shouting *two-for-one*!"

She knew this story. Of course she did. It had happened way back when Dalton was a kid, and he got a lot of mileage out of it. But she laughed anyway, because she loved to hear him tell it.

"That's ridiculous," Jessie said, wiping a tear underneath her eye. "What are the chances?"

"They must not be very good, because I've never known another person that it happened to. And it never happened to him again."

"He was just lucky I guess," Cassidy said, smiling at him.

"I guess so," he responded. "I know I am."

And she tried to pick that apart. To see if there was anything underlying those words. A secret message that was meant only for her. Or something.

Jessie sighed heavily and looked at her phone. "I have to start another round again. Just pounding out a shoe, but look, there's a crowd coming."

"You look tired," Cassidy said, meaning to be helpful.

But Jessie flinched. "Do I?"

"Not in a bad way," Cassidy said hurriedly. "In a way that suggests you're very industrious."

Her older brother Flynn reached over and clapped his hand on her shoulder. "Quit while you're only a little bit behind, Cass."

Cassidy felt her smile falter. "Can I help with anything?"

"You can go gather some people," Jessie said.

"I will," she said, scampering away and finding a knot of teenagers. "There's a blacksmithing demonstration starting over there. Free to watch."

She moved through the group of people, marveling at all the strange faces. So many people drove all the way out to Rustler Mountain around the holidays. It was a local tourist attraction. The kind of place that was worth an hour's drive.

Sometimes Cassidy wondered what it would be like to live close to a movie theater, a chain restaurant or a Walmart, instead of being well over an hour away. But her ultimate conclusion was that it just wasn't the life for her.

She liked living here. The sense of community, the traditions.

She had no intention of leaving. She liked stability. The familiarity of Rustler Mountain. The sameness of life here.

Well, a lot of things in her life had changed lately, but *she* had no intention of changing.

Except, she did want things to change with Dalton. It was what she had always hoped for.

And if he rejects you, then what?

No. She'd had enough bad things happen to her. She had been over this in her mind before. If you were abandoned by your mother, brought to a town you had never even heard of to live with your father, who died right before you arrived, leaving you totally stranded with three feral older brothers, then you were owed some smooth sailing.

She was convinced of that. Or rather, she wanted to be convinced of that.

She gathered quite a crowd to visit the booth, where she watched her brother admiring Jessie's handiwork.

"She's something," said Flynn.

The way he looked at his fiancée, it was just so obvious he was head over heels in love. It was really something. It brought her back to that earlier interaction with Dalton. What had she seen in his eyes?

She couldn't be sure.

But then, nothing ventured, nothing gained.

She turned her focus on Jessie, who was heating the horseshoe, bringing it out of the forge when it was bright red, and hammering it forcefully, the sound of metal on metal filling the air.

Jessie went on until the shoe was the perfect shape, then doused it in water, cooling it. She gave it to a triumphant little girl in the front row.

"I didn't know girls could do jobs like that," the little girl said.

"Of course we can," said Jessie. "And I'm also going to be the mayor of this town. We can do anything we put our minds to."

Cassidy smiled. Because the exchange was adorable. And honestly, it just made her proud to call Jessie part of the family. Funny, because Jessie was a Hancock, and only two years ago, her older brother Austin would have had a heart attack if he'd been told that a Hancock was going to marry into his family.

Wilder family lore was deep and vast. Well, the lore of this entire town was like that. Founded during the gold rush, Rustler Mountain had been filled with pioneers, both good and bad. When Austin had started doing deep historical research into their family roots, it turned out that the ones who had been touted as heroic for years were somewhat more complex.

For years town lore had been all about the heroes and the villains. The outlaws and the lawmen. And of course, the Wilder family had been among the outlaws.

Her brother was named after Austin Wilder, who had been a stagecoach and train robber, notorious throughout the state of Oregon for his crimes. He had ridden with his two brothers and a fourth gang member named Butch Hancock. Until Lee Talbot, sheriff of Rustler Mountain, had shot Austin Wilder dead in the street and had the other Wilders hanged for suspicion of murder.

But it turned out that Lee Talbot had colluded with Butch Hancock, agreeing to give him immunity if the sheriff could have the notoriety of taking down Oregon's most notorious gang. The Wilders had been criminals, but they had never committed murder.

Austin had set the record straight in his best-selling book, and Millie had started setting the record straight throughout town, which had led to a lot of historical inaccuracies and half-truths being corrected. Now the true history of the town could be told, not just by the victors—white men who liked to claim ultimate authority—but the stories of Chinese immigrants, of Black settlers who had met with hostility and been kept out of the state because of virulently racist laws, and of course the Native American tribes whose land had been taken from them.

So maybe things did change. And some of them definitely needed to.

She looked over at Dalton.

And then the atmosphere around the booth changed. Shifted. As if the air itself shivered.

She turned because she was compelled, like steel to a magnet. And not just her apparently, because every head turned.

West Hancock had just arrived. He wasn't dressed seasonally.

He wore a tight black T-shirt, muscular arms on display for no reason. Black ink licked up his forearms, past his biceps and disappeared beneath the sleeves of the shirt.

He also wore a black cowboy hat, black jeans, black boots.

He was, without a doubt, the only man in town with a more dangerous reputation than her brothers . . .

www.ingramcontent.com/pod-product-compliance
Lightning Source LLC
LaVergne TN
LVHW030911080826
845145LV00010B/2850

* 9 7 8 1 4 9 6 7 5 6 5 7 2 *